# BLACK
# FANG

## MIRIKA MAYO
## CORNELIUS

# BLACK FANG

This is a work of fiction. Names, characters, places and incidents are either products of the author's imagination or are used fictitiously. Any resemblance to actual events or locales or persons, living or dead, is entirely coincidental.

Copyright © Mirika Mayo Cornelius, June 2023
ISBN: 978-1-946870-15-5

An Akirim Press Publishing
Book Cover by Mirika Mayo Cornelius
www.akirimpress.com

# Acknowledgements

To God be the glory. He allows me to share this story. Bless the Father, the Son Jesus and the Holy Ghost.

Thanks to all who have supported me in my family and beyond.

# Dedication

This story is dedicated to my son.

# BLACK FANG

Bailey lives a normal teenage life - fun in school, a best friend and goals for the future - until the day her father passes away. She discovers that she's different from everyone else, different in ways that she doesn't want to confront, but she has no choice, especially when her deceased father reveals the mission that she must complete. If she fails, it may cost her life, but even if she completes the mission, she remains bound to the possibility of losing something she holds so dear ... forever.

# Table of Contents

# BLACK FANG

Black Fang

# Black Fang | Chapter One

"I'm up! I'm up! Mom, you can stop calling me now. I just hit snooze and accidently went back to sleep," she calls, answering the shouts of her punctual mother as she throws the lightweight sheet from her body which sweat all night long due to the air conditioning unit being broken.

"Well, don't forget to come straight back home from school because our entire cool night rests on you being back here to let the HVAC man in here to bring us some cool air," she yells from the front door as Bailey rushes to her bedroom door to wave goodbye to her mother.

"Okay, Ma. I love you, and have a good day. I'll come straight back. Daddy already left?"

"Yeah, he had to leave early. He'll be back on Thursday. He has a long haul to the other side of the country. I love you, sweetheart," she says, tossing her purse onto her shoulder, blowing a kiss to her only daughter and leaving the three-bedroom, single story brick house which went up for sale some weeks back. "Come lock the door for me!" she shouts upon exit.

Bailey drags to the front door in her long, purple pajama shirt damp with sweat, and locks the door, feeling miserable. Sure, the air conditioning unit is broken, but she thinks to herself, would that make her feel so nauseous? Holding her stomach, she creeps into the kitchen to grab a thirst quenching drink, remembering how she felt last year which is similar to how she felt last year running for the Prestine Academy High School's track team.

"I'm probably dehydrated. I did sweat overnight," she mumbles, as she takes a sip of the drink before feeling disgusted for not brushing her teeth first. "Nope, this is not gonna work. I feel like I just drank a tub full of bacteria. Gross." As she twists the cap back onto the drink, her hand violently shakes, wasting the entire drink onto the floor. It splashes everywhere, and the worst part is that her mother just mopped the kitchen floor last night before bed.

"Oh no. Just great," she complains, ignoring her tremors and quickly yanking the kitchen towel from the refrigerator to wipe up the orange mess that flows across the floor. After cleaning it up, she rushes to the back in order to slip into the shower and brush her teeth at the same time. The shower, along with a fresh clean mouth, makes her feel much better, so she slides into what she considers an amazing outfit for school. It's School Spirit Week, and she decided on the perfect look for Celebrity/Decade Theme Day. As she pulls her hair back to put on the long, full brown wig, she feels a powerful, spasmic tug at the front of her mouth.

"Ouch," she gasps as she curiously runs her tongue across her front teeth and gums. They taste funny, almost like she didn't brush her teeth at all. Although they appear fine, they feel full of pits and even rough, like they're caked with some thick film. Therefore, she quickly put on the wig and re-brushes her teeth before doing her light makeup. "Mom is gonna flip when I send her these pics of me rocking out in the eighties," she smiles, having grabbed all her ideas online, from the big, asymmetric hair styles to bangles around her wrists.

As she turns to take a couple more pictures before heading out, she places them in a text message to her father and hits send with the message telling him that she loves him. She finishes getting ready only twenty minutes before school starts and bolts from the house, leaving her breakfast shake in the refrigerator. "Dang it!" She's too late though, so instead of going back inside, she jumps from the porch, knocks down the for sale sign in the front yard and rushes to school in her Spirit Week costume. "They're not gonna sell my house."

# Black Fang | Chapter Two

"Why didn't I do the eighties? You have the big hair and all with the bracelets up the arm!"

"Because I got the brains, and you got the body to pull off what you're doing," Bailey answers jokingly as she adores her best friend Delight's seventies costume, complete with an afro and skin tight bell bottoms. The two made a game of guessing what costume the other would wear, and both guessed wrong.

"And I look good with my fro and hoops!" her friend adds.

"If I didn't know better, I'd think we're about to have *the* concert of the year. I mean, we look good!" Bailey says admiring everyone in the hall dressed as their favorite celebrities. There's supposed to be a group picture where all of those dressed up will meet after homeroom attendance, and Bailey's been posing in the mirror for days in an attempt to give flawless face to the camera. "I'll see you after homeroom, okay, for pictures?"

"Yeah. Fix your hair," she answers, reaching over to toss Bailey's wig to the side. "You know if it wasn't big in the eighties, it wasn't right!" she laughs.

"Right! The bangs were ten feet tall!" she jokes as they part ways, giggling to their assigned homerooms and excited about Celebrity/Decade Day. However, before Bailey gets there, an odd taste begins to spread on the right side of her mouth. It's not only an odd taste, but it's also warm, so immediately, she detours to the girl's bathroom. A couple of girls are already in there, so she remains as calm as she can in order not to draw unwanted attention while her mouth fills with what she now recognizes as blood. She enters the stall, locks it and stares into the toilet. What's staring back at her from inside the toilet is not good, so good, so she exits and enters another stall. Finally, the other girls leave, and she's alone. Lifting her finger, she wipes the edge of her lip, grazing the fluid as she prays it isn't what she thinks it is, and then lifts her wet finger directly in front of her face. It's blood.

Panicked nearly to hyperventilating from the uncertainty of what's going on, she spits blood from her mouth, but it just keeps coming, not from her throat but from what feels like her gums. Even more petrified, she continues to spit, pulling her costume wig back from her face, but each time she shuts her mouth, the bleeding doesn't stop. Finally, she flushes the toilet and leaves the stall, bolting straight to the mirror, and as she smiles, her reflection delivers horror. Within seconds, Bailey is on her smartphone frantically searching for the word she has become accustomed to hearing on toothpaste commercials – gingivitis. The warning school bell sounds, causing her to shake her phone impatiently as the browser loads.

"Come on, come on!" The results of the search finally pop up. "Gingivitis is bleeding gums and can be a sign of periodontal disease?" she stresses, her eyes bulging at the amount of horrible information and pictures compiled on the screen. She removes her eyes from the screen and takes several slow, deep breaths.

"Look one more time." Facing the mirror, she gathers the courage to open her mouth, and after about five seconds, she smiles. The whites of her teeth turn red from streaks of blood rapidly exiting her gums.

"That's it. I'm going home." She spits the blood into the sink, rinses it out and then, storms from the bathroom. When the last bell sounds, she races from the school before she has to face anyone. Checking her pockets for change, she finds some cash that will allow her to catch the city bus back home, but when she feels the blood stream into her mouth once again, she alters that plan, deciding to walk. It takes her about thirty minutes to arrive, and the whole way home, she spit blood. Not only that, she also discovers something worse - her teeth are loose.

Multiple calls come in to her cell phone, and she knows why. She's missing from school, and she figures it's Delight without even looking. After she shuts and locks the door behind her, she tosses her book bag and cell phone to the side chair and runs to the bathroom. "Mouthwash. That's all I need is mouthwash." She reaches beneath the sink and gratefully finds it. There's a little left, and she's confident she will make it count. "That's what the internet says, to floss and rinse, so that's what I'm gonna do," she continues as she pours a half capful of mouthwash, trying her best not to waste what's left. Then, she carefully pours it all in her mouth after spitting more blood into the porcelain sink.

The second the mouthwash touches her gums, an excruciating pain rips through what feels like every area of her mouth. Throwing her mouth beneath the faucet, she rinses with cold water for about one full minute as the pain slowly subsides. Then, she backs into the bathroom wall in full out fear and confusion. "What's wrong with my mouth?" she cries as she taps the outside of her cheeks, feeling her teeth move with each touch. Trembling, she decides to call her mother, so she goes back into the living room to retrieve her phone. When she picks it up, it starts ringing in her hand. It's Delight.

"Hello?" Bailey answers, her voice uncontrollably quivering.

"Bailey, what's wrong?" she asks, gathering by her friend's voice that something isn't quite right. "Where are you? We took the pics for Spirit Week already, and you were literally nowhere to be found. You weren't answering your phone, and you sound like you're crying? You alright?"

"Delight, I uh…" she pauses to gather her thoughts, "something's wrong with me."

"What do you mean? Where are you, so I can come to you?"

"No, no, I'm at home."

"Home?"

"I had to leave," Bailey responds, afraid to say what is going on inside her mouth. Watching the blood drip onto her cell phone, she wipes her mouth, and her level of anxiety increases to a point that she helplessly and hopelessly drops herself to the floor. "I dunno what's wrong, Delight!"

"Bailey!" she worries, obviously losing it because she doesn't understand anything that's going on. Ever since she moved into the city with her mother, it was Bailey who helped her become acclimated with the new area and people. To her,

Bailey isn't just a best friend but a sister to whom she's grown a strong bond with after the passing of her father which is the reason her and her mother left their previous home. The home just wasn't ever the same, and the relocation was the best thing that happened to Delight, giving her a glimmer of hope for the future again.

"I don't know, Dee!" she answers, calling her Dee for short. "My mouth…"

"What about your mouth?"

"It won't stop bleeding."

"Bleeding?" she asks in disbelief.

"Yes, Dee. Bleeding."

"I'm skipping school. I'm coming. Did you call your mom?"

"I was just going to. My dad is gone, and we don't bother him with emergencies that we can handle when he's on the road. Mom forbids me from stressing him out when he's already…"

"Well, listen. Call your mom, and I'm still headed over, okay?"

"Yeah."

"And don't worry about it. I'm coming."

"Okay. Thanks, Dee."

"See you soon."

# Black Fang | Chapter Three

"I don't know what's wrong with me," Bailey whimpers as the call ends, leaving her severely stressed and weak. Her vision blurs while she stumbles toward the front door, deciding to leave it unlocked just in case she can't make it back to the door. From there, she stumbles back to the bathroom where she takes her nausea out in the toilet before intense pains travel through her neck and face, climaxing through her jawbone and gums.

Throwing herself against the cool, white-tiled wall, she applies pressure to her neck in an attempt to stop the magnificent spasm that seems to be taking her young life. She can't speak, and at the same time her voice departs, she goes completely blind. The darkness and the pain throw her into turmoil as she pulls at her pulsating mouth. Streams of blood seep through her fingers like water from a fountain, and it pours from the palms of her hands and down her neck like a spilled bucket of red paint. Tremors run through her body creating an uncontrollable, seizure-like volatility until suddenly,

Bailey collapses, banging her head onto the bathroom rug. At that point, nothing exists, and as she sinks further into darkness, the scent of her father mysteriously creeps by before she's out cold.

"Bailey! Bailey!" Delight shouts, banging on the front door before discovering that it's already open. This creates a worse concern, and she runs through the sweltering house, frantically searching for her best friend. "Bailey, answer me!"

She stares down the hallway at Bailey's room door. It's shut, and she hears nothing. Gripped with fear of the unknown, possibly that Bailey's near death or even dead, she bolts back toward the multicolored, art-plastered bedroom door and shoves it open to find a calm Bailey sitting at her desk with headphones on listening to something on her computer. The music is so loud that Delight hears the beat through the headphones.

Furious, she snatches the headphones from Bailey's head. "Do you think that was funny? I skipped school, took public transportation here, and there's absolutely nothing wrong with you that I can see, Bailey. Is this a joke because who's laughing?"

Bailey doesn't turn around despite the headphones being ripped from her ears. Instead, she sits there in her black and white gamer chair without the slightest hint of being disturbed, staring at the computer screen before answering Delight. "I feel fine now. I was about to call you back, but I knew you were on your way. There was no need."

Standing there perturbed, Delight shouts, "Well turn around! Where's all this blood? Let me see your mouth."

Bailey swivels around to face her best friend. "See," she smiles, her teeth just as white and normal as this morning in school. "There's nothing wrong anymore. I think I may have cut it and shouldn'tve made it worse by rinsing it with mouthwash. Everything's all dried up."

"What about all of what you said? Lift your lips up, Bailey. Smile wider."

"I'm alright, Delight," she ignores her, swiveling her chair back around, quite dismissive of her purposely. Delight notices, but can't place her finger on what is really going on. Therefore, instead of saying anything else, she inspects the bedroom. Everything is in order, but then she notices the back of Bailey's head. Bailey sits there with her hair in a pony tail. There's no sign of the big eighties wig she wore in school, and she isn't wearing the full costume anymore either. To Delight, something is definitely suspicious, so she cautiously continues with her line of questioning because it appears as if Bailey isn't returning to school despite being all better.

"Why did you change so fast? If everything is alright," she asks, backing up to look down the hallway again, "where are your clothes? I got here in less than thirty minutes, and you were clearly messed up when..."

"It was a cut," she sharply interrupts, not willing to discuss it until she understands what's going on with her body ever since she got up from the bathroom floor. She spins back around in her chair and walks over to Delight to show her face clearer. "See. Look at me." She places her hands on

Delight's shoulders. "And my costume, it's over there in the dirty clothes. I took it off because I told you, I rinsed my mouth, and a mess got all over it when spit it out. See," she explains, going over to the laundry basket to lift the least bloody piece of clothing into full sight.

Still paranoid like there's more to the story, Delight lowers her eyes and nods. "Yeah, I see. You should've called me back and let me know. I need to get back to school. Since you feel better, are you coming? I mean, it's too hot in here to stay home all day. You might get sick again, right...from this heat?"

"Nah. I'm gonna sit around here. I'll see you tomorrow, okay?"

Delight watches as Bailey takes her seat once again, completely at a loss as to what is happening with her friend. She's never gotten the cold shoulder from her, and she's nearly certain Bailey is hiding something. However, because she needs to get back to school, she escorts herself out of the front door, but as she's leaving, she notices a very small drop of what looks like fresh blood on the floor beneath the door knob. She turns back to see if Bailey is behind her, but no one is there. Then, she curiously leans over and touches the top of the blood bubble with the tip of her index finger. A fiery jolt races through her fingertip, up her spine and then directly into her brain, causing a quick temporary lapse of consciousness, however, she doesn't collapse. She regains stamina rather quickly, glances at her finger once more, shakes off whatever it was that made her light-headed and then leaves to make her way back to school. Meanwhile, Bailey stands at her bedroom doorway. She'd watched the entire thing unbeknownst to Delight but not because she wanted to watch. It's because she somehow felt an insatiable urge to watch. As soon as Delight touched her blood, Bailey felt it, too, and what she felt, she didn't like at all because it's not normal to feel someone else touch your own blood.

# Black Fang | Chapter Four

With a floral napkin, Bailey wipes that last drop of blood from the floor that was touched by Delight, and she replays everything that has happened this morning, from her gums bleeding to Delight coming over and how it felt when she touched her blood. The most challenging thing to grasp though is the new set of teeth that have oddly grown in her mouth out of nowhere.

Quickly, she walks to the bathroom, flushes the napkin down the toilet and faces the mirror. She then rubs her tongue across her teeth. They appear exactly the same as before, but she's consumed with why there are two brand new sets of canines in her mouth.

All of her other original teeth are gone. What she thought would be her permanent teeth, she's collected and hid beneath her mattress after they fell out onto the bathroom floor during her black out. She woke up to all of them on the floor, quickly hid them in a towel, blood and all, where no one would think to look. Her new set of teeth look the exact same way as her other set of teeth except stronger. She can even feel her blood lightly pulsating through the roots of the newly formed teeth. Before, her teeth were slightly sensitive, but now, they feel abnormally healthy, like beyond healthy.

There's a small mirror in the bathroom drawer that she uses from time to time from an old makeup case. She slides it out of the drawer and holds it up to her mouth for a closer inspection. Then, she angles the mirror beneath her top jaw, struggling to get the proper angle to look into her mouth and examine her new teeth. She can feel a second set of canine teeth, but she can't see them. It feels like they are hidden behind the other ones.

"Come on..." she struggles until finally, there they are, and seeing them is different from feeling them. The tips are much sharper than the other visible canines, and they even feel much different than regular bone. Seeing them made everything an awful reality, and she freezes, dropping the mirror onto the countertop. From there, it slips from the counter to the floor, breaking to pieces. She stares at herself through the broken pieces, and as she picks up each piece, she senses something is very different now, more than just having new fangs. It's deeper, much deeper than the roots of any fangs can reach, and it's pulsating through her soul.

"Ouch," Delight complains as she squeezes the palm of her right hand which is suffering from a terrible, unexplainable throbbing. The people on the bus gawk her way strangely, and some pull out their cellular phones to record. Delight behaves as if she doesn't see them, convincing herself that the hoopla is all about her costume. When the bus stops, a couple of people move by her to exit, finally realizing that she is in severe pain. However, they only whisper to each other as they get off the bus, staring back in concern.

The pain circulating through the palm of her hand worsens, expanding its territory to her wrist and elbow. Therefore, she leans forward, placing her head into her lap in order to stabilize her arm in between her body so she won't burst into tears. Agony encompasses her entire right arm, and she begins to tremble from the pain. That's when the city bus stops again near the high school, but she doesn't get off. Instead, she decides to go straight home because she needs to be at home. Something's wrong.

When the bus reaches the closest stop to her neighborhood, she exits and makes a terribly, painful trek home. No one is in the neighborhood at all because everyone on the main street works a full-time job. She lives only five homes from the main road, and the bed is all she wants along with some pain relievers.

By the time she makes it to the door, the pain is nearly unbearable, and her hand is curling up like it's severely arthritic. Each joint feels like they're fractured.

"What's wrong with me?" she weeps as she struggles to open the door. A pulsating vibration runs through her arm, and there's a torturous pain at the tip of her finger, the same finger she used to touch Bailey's blood. She stumbles down the hallway, but before she makes it to her bedroom, she takes a hard fall onto the freshly-cleaned, beige carpet and goes partially unconscious, entering into what feels and looks like another dimension.

In her dazed state, there's a figure of man whose silhouette is familiar. It's as if she's met the man somewhere before but doesn't quite know until he walks closer to her, moving out of the shadows. Her arm, still binding her in insatiable discomfort, now has an unbearable heaviness, and as she struggles to push herself from the floor, she finally recognizes who the man is who is now directly in front of her. Tears flow from her eyes, and all the agony in her arm no longer matters. The man before her is her late father, and he's kneeling to meet her in her struggle.

"Daddy?" she whimpers in disbelief.

"Delight," his voice echoes as he speaks inside an empty chamber, and it sounds just as she remembers it which causes her to inconsolably weep because she misses him so much. He was brutally murdered, and his killer was never caught. That's been a moment of constant despair for her and her mother, the unknown and even the why. Nothing has ever been solved nor has anything made sense. As he kneels before her, she tries to reach for him, but she can't move her arm at all anymore.

"Daddy, something's wrong with me. I can't move, dad. It hurts," she cries, terrified of what is becoming of her, believing that she's dying herself because she's in the presence of her father. "Am I dying? What's wrong with me?"

"Nothing's wrong with you, baby girl. It's what's meant to be. You will see, and you will complete it. Tell no one you saw me, Delight. No one."

"What? What's meant to be?" she asks confused, but as she asks, he stands to his feet again and starts to back away. "Daddy, don't leave me. Don't leave me, please. Help me, dad, please! Don't leave me again!" she pleads, but his smile disappears, turning into a cold seriousness before he fades back into his silhouette of nothingness. "Daddy!" she continuously screams until she passes out, awakening a couple hours later to confusion.

Her arm is no longer in debilitating pain, and despite being inside her own home, she's lost, unable to come to grips with where she was when she saw her father and what is actually happening. "Daddy," she calls, not knowing whether or not the vision she had was real.

Suddenly, her cell phone starts to send off multiple alerts, so she gets up from the floor, grabs her phone but is taken aback at how swift she's moving. She feels like she's gliding, and as she notices the time, she spins around, "Two hours? I was there for that long?"

Instead of checking what looks like the hundredth message on her cell phone, she ignores them in order to call her mom. However, when she goes to dial, something knocks the phone from her hand, causing it to fly to the other side of the hallway. Frightened, she backs into the bathroom, slamming the door shut and backing toward the shower, but pauses in pure horror when she notices the side of her face in the mirror's reflection, causing her to fall backwards into the tub devastated.

"What the...?" she asks herself, questioning what she saw as she rubs the side of her face, feeling multiple, minute rash like bumps all over it. Suddenly, everything blurs as she watches the bathroom door morph into the shape of a body.

She screams, "Get away from me!" as she furiously wipes her eyes in an attempt to clear her vision when in seconds, everything goes back to normal. Terrified and confused, she hugs her knees to her chest as the only way to protect herself from what may be attacking her. "What's wrong with me? What's wrong with my face?" she asks, lightly touching what has become like scales on the right side of her face. She sinks down further into the bathtub and weeps, severely depressed about her unusually cryptic situation, for hours.

# Black Fang | Chapter Five

"Who is it?" Bailey asks at the ring of the doorbell.

"I'm the HVAC man ...your air conditioning..."

"Come on inside," she responds, opening the front door. "I opened the gate though if you want to head out to it. It's around back. The other half is in the attic...but I'm sure you know that."

"Yeah, I do. It's my specialty. I'm gonna put this here if you don't mind and swing around to the backyard for a second. Will you do me a favor and turn the thermostat on and then off again. I just wanna hear it come on."

"No problem. Anything else?"

"Nope. That'll be it. Hopefully, we can get it nice and cool in here for you in no time, he answers, straining to bend over and retrieve his pen that dropped to the floor. He's a short, slim, middle-aged man with a thinning hair line and freckles all around his nose. "I'm surprised you can stand it in here. It's a death trap. I'm already sweating, and look at you. You look," he pauses, "cold."

"I do?"

"Yeah, you do? Are you feeling okay?" he asks extremely concerned at the pasty, matte appearance of what should be her normal, slightly oily, lively teenage brown skin.

"Yeah, I uh…" she stutters as she glances at the living room mirror before twisting back his way in pure shock. Her face looks like a wax doll. "You can start now. I'll hit the thermostat," she urges him so she can tend to her ghastly appearance.

When she turns to walk away, what she didn't notice before, she notices now. Her body temperature plummets as she comes to the realization that her body temperature is off – way off. Fighting hard not to shiver because she's aware that he's probably still watching her out of concern, she raises her hand to flip the thermostat, but her fingernails are turning a dark blue, so she quickly turns to him and asks, "Problem?"

He becomes startled and jumps to answer. "No, uh, no…just making sure you're okay is all. You seem to be shaking a bit like you're ... are you diabetic? Because I am. I have some juice in the van that I can share..."

"I'm fine," she stutters as her teeth chatter. "Go on. Flu. Don't get too close."

"Yeah, sure, yeah..." he agrees as he steps away from the front door. "I'll be back inside to go into the attic. If it's what I think it might be, it won't be too long." He then leaves from her presence to perform his duties. Meanwhile, Bailey's fingers have already started turning a deep purple at their tips, like she's in the process of turning into a zombie.

She races to her bedroom, shuts the door and crawls beneath the layers of cover she'd placed atop the bed prior to the HVAC man coming to house. This makes her body temperature do the opposite of what she wants. It gets even colder!

"What's wrong with me?" she asks herself as she tries to warm up. It's obvious the house is sweltering beneath the heat of the blazing sun but her body is as cold as an icy sidewalk on a winter day. As she lies beneath the cover, she continues to ponder what's going on until she figures out that maybe she should make herself cooler to make her body temperature go in the opposite direction.

Her blinds and window are wide open from where she made the effort to get some air or a light breeze in. Unfortunately, it may be making the room hotter, so she shuts it and pulls the curtain. Within seconds, nothing happens. Frustrated, she puts together some sheets of notebook paper and fans herself viciously like she's in church on a hot Sunday morning until she starts feeling what she's waiting on - internal warmth.

"Oh my gosh! It's working," she says, running into her mom's master bath to run cold water in her hands. Her fingernails and palms go from the dark blue, purplish color to the white and light brown. "I can't believe this. Extremely hot temperatures are making me cold, and that would mean that extremely cold temperatures would make me hot."

She burst through the bedroom door, about to run down the hallway, until the HVAC man comes stomping down the attic stairs before her very eyes. She scoots around the attic stairs, realizing that he's watching her oddly but out of concern, and goes to plant herself in front of the freezer to get some ice cream...or pretend to get some. It's the only way to create a balance in her body's core temperature, or at least she believes it is. The only way to know is to test it out.

"Come on science class. Be good for something," she hopes as she sticks her head inside the freezer, and sure enough, her theory is correct. Standing at the open freezer helps to level her core body temperature, and she decides to leave it open...and stand there scooping out ice cream ... until the air conditioning unit is fixed.

The HVAC repair man walks by the kitchen towards the front door, lowering his head to the side in order to check on her because he's still concerned, and Bailey smiles back with a spoonful of ice cream high in the air in order to convince him she's okay. He gives her a thumbs up, sighs and continues on his way, thankful that she's finally getting some sugar in her system. "I'll be right back in. I have one more thing to do before I turn your thermostat back on, and it should be good to go."

"Bailey, you alright in here, honey? It's me, Mrs. Conyers from across the street. Your mom told me to check on you, keep an eye out while the air conditioning unit is getting fixed," she shouts from the front door as the repair man scoots by her.

Bailey drops her spoon inside the container of ice cream and hurries to the front door. "Yes ma'am. Thanks for checking on me. I'm fine, just eating some ice cream to get warm, I mean, keep cool."

"Well, I'm out here on the porch until he's gone. If you need me, knock on that window or call me. You have my cell phone number. I'm right there from my porch watching."

"As you always have, Mrs. Conyers," Bailey answers sarcastically and under her breath with a huge smile. "If something goes wrong, though, I'll get your attention fast."

"And leave this door open. Here," she says adjusting the screen door so that it remains open. "There. Just holler."

"Yes ma'am."

"You sure you alright?" She stops to inspect Bailey from head to toe. "You look like you got into a fight or something. Is that why I saw you come home so early from school today? You been here since then, child? You been here all day. I saw a young lady walk off from ..."

"A fight?" Bailey interjects, wondering what's wrong with her face now. "No ma'am, I uhh..."

"Yeah, it's a black eye," Mrs. Conyers confirms to herself. "Thing turning purple right before my very eyes. Go put some ice on that, wrap the ice up in a rag or drop it in two socks, wrap it round in a knot and sit it on your eye. Look like you getting two black eyes. Your mama won't be pleased. Your mom know you been home all day long?"

"Oh! Oh... no... uh... that's magic makeup for art class. I'm doing metamorphosis makeup. Gotta go, Mrs. Conyers!"

"I ain't never heard of that kinda makeup before..."

"I'll holler really loud if I need you! I have to go before it turns even more purple," Bailey lies, leaving the door wide open and Mrs. Conyers standing there peeking inside the house. She stops at the entrance to the kitchen, takes a deep breath and shouts, "I'm fine, Mrs. Conyers! Bye!"

Mrs. Conyers then rushes off away from the house and back across the street. Meanwhile, Bailey shoves her entire head into the freezer. It's one minute later that the air conditioning repairman comes back inside the house, turns on the thermostat and cautiously walks back over to the kitchen where he notices Bailey's head mimicking frozen meat.

"Excuse me?" he calls.

Startled, Bailey bangs her head on the freezer rack as she backs away to face the repairman. He considers asking her why she had her head stuffed inside the freezer, but he assumes it's from the heat and doesn't. "I'm all done. I've tested it, and now all that needs to be done is the payment."

"Sure. Mom left the money. I just have to grab it and get the receipt. How much?"

"Three hundred and fifty dollars. Uh, but I need an adult to sign this real quick. I thought your mom would be here for..."

"Oh no but... Mrs. Conyers!" Bailey shouts through the screen door. As soon as Mrs. Conyers hears her name, she springs into action, crossing the street once again, heading over to save the day.

"Yes, Bailey! I'm coming. I'm coming."

"Will you sign for mom?" Bailey asks as Mrs. Conyers approaching. "She left the money, and I guess she didn't think about my having to sign any paperwork."

Mrs. Conyers steps into the home out of breath. "I'll sign it as soon as I know this air is working. Is the cool air coming out?"

"Yes ma'am. You can reach up and feel it for yourself," the repairman confidently answers.

"Well, then, here's my signature. You have the money, or do I need to front it before your mom gets back?"

"No, I have the money," she repeats because it's obvious Mrs. Conyers didn't hear her the first time, "... and thank you."

She looks at Bailey strangely, but doesn't say anything until after she signs all the paperwork and the repairman leaves. As the door shuts behind him, she turns back to Bailey and comments, "I don't see where you have a black eye or two anymore. It really must have been make-up."

"Oh, I washed it off...most of it. Some might be on there. I did it fast because I had to pay the..."

"If you say so." She takes a deep breath before glancing around the living room and heading out the door. "I'll send your mother a message. Tell her all is well. You contact her, too. All moms want to hear their babies are okay, so you do that. I'm surprised she isn't pulling up yet. She's normally round the corner by now."

Bailey watches the healthy, athletic senior lady walk back across the street. Not only is she in great shape, but her mind is super sharp. She never misses anything because she's always looking out the blinds or sitting on the porch. Nothing gets past her, and if it does, she puts the missing pieces together like a puzzle.

As Bailey shuts the door, she puts on not only the screen lock, but all the locks, including the chain lock, on the front door. Finally, she takes a deep breath and leans her back against the door while sliding slowly to the floor.

"I can't go back to school like this tomorrow," she complained, frustrated as she stands from the floor to position herself in front of the newly flowing air, being sure to set the temperature to a nice medium. "I hope this all goes away," she sulks as her body temperature returns to normal. About one hour later, the home is cool, but when her mom walks in near seven o'clock, which is much later for her, she is in tears.

# Black Fang | Chapter Six

"Mom? Mom!" Bailey calls, rushing to the living room, dismissing everything that happened to her earlier in order to tend to her mother who appears devastated. She's never seen her mom so distraught, so she continues to press her mother about what's wrong. "Mom, what's wrong? What's the matter? Please, tell me," Bailey pleads, but her mom doesn't answer. She only removes her work shoes and the makeup from her eyes with her bare hands as the tears stream down her cheeks. Then, she stares a Bailey like she's never seen her a day in her life before apologizing profusely.

"Ma? Ma, what? Why are you apologizing?" Bailey begins to cry along with her mother, but as the tears flow, they oddly steam on her cheeks, and she quickly wipes them away with her shirt. "Come on, Ma. It's gonna be okay no matter what it is," she says in order to remain confident and combat whatever is upsetting her mother. "Do you need me to call dad?"

Bailey stands to retrieve her cellular phone, but her mom grabs her by the wrist to stop her. Upon touching her daughter, she senses something different about Bailey's skin, but when she glances down, everything appears fine, so she continues, "Sit, baby."

Bailey slowly takes a seat next to her mother, and immediately, she knows something horrible has happened to her father. "It's dad?"

"Yeah, baby. It's him."

"Mama," Bailey cries, "Don't tell me."

"He got into a bad accident earlier today. The truck tipped and uh…"

"Mama," Bailey calls, shaking her head and moving from the couch.

"He didn't make it, honey. Your father's gone…from us. He's gone."

Bailey screams at the top of her lungs, releasing so much unbearable anguish that even when her mom tries to console her, Bailey tips the coffee table that sits in the middle of the room, and everything flies from it onto the other side of the wall. Her mother falls back onto the sofa, wailing and reaching out, trying to calm her distraught daughter, however, nothing works. Bailey is out of control, and her mother has no idea the level.

In seconds, Bailey storms off back to the room, slamming her door, and as her mom gets on her cell phone to call a friend for help, Bailey has already begun destroying everything in her room, everything except the family portrait that was taken last year. She stops the destruction, yielding to the sight of her father in the picture and reaching out to touch his face. However, when her finger touches the glass instead, she flies into a rage once again before exiting the bedroom window to head to the backyard. It's there where she hides in her father's storage unit and weeps beside his last wooden project – an eagle in flight.

"Daddy," she weeps, remembering everything she can about him, his deep voice to the way he laughed and joked. It's here were she sleeps all night. Her mother never disturbs her because she doesn't know how to fix the situation or make the loss less painful. She walks into Bailey's bedroom and is left in shock at the way she ripped through everything. She starts cleaning it up as much as she can to keep herself sane, and when she's done, instead of sleeping in the house, as the night falls upon the earth, she takes her rest outside underneath the stars in order to protect her daughter. She never sleeps. She only weeps.

# Black Fang | Chapter Seven

There's thunder but no rain on the day of the funeral. It's a closed casket, and everyone around Bailey is dressed in black. Bailey, however, she dressed in blue. Blue was her dad's favorite color. Her mother sits beside her confounded by everything and everyone. Naturally, she hasn't been the same since the news of his death, and Bailey, though people visited the home day and night after the news broke of his passing, there is still a feeling of loneliness. It's her first time feeling internal emptiness.

She glances over at Delight who stands only four feet away from her, ready to come to her aid if she needs it like a true friend. Then, she glances at her mother once again, before they are both ushered toward the casket which is elevated over the hole into which her father will be lowered. Bouquets of flowers are everywhere, and Bailey doesn't feel good about them at all. She doesn't want them there. She doesn't want any of this. All she wants is her father, but she now fully realizes that she'll never have him again.

As she cries at the lowering of the casket, she can't rid herself of the feeling that all her tears are for nothing. Crying won't bring him back just like the destruction of her room didn't bring him back, therefore, she ignores the saltiness of her annoying tears that drape her face like they aren't supposed to dry up. Refusing to touch them, Bailey holds her head down, listening to the preacher announce that all is well with her dad's soul. All is well with his soul.

"But what about mine?"

As her words force dominion over all the other sounds at the gravesite, the preacher goes silent, but Bailey doesn't look up. Like fingertips all over her body, she can literally feel the stares of the crowd, and it causes her to fight back, not against them but against the pain and unexplained end to her father. "Does anyone have the answer to that? *I'm* left here. What about *my* soul? *I'm* not alright." Bailey knows she isn't okay mentally. Her mind is in a place where it's never been, and it's making her afraid. There was never life without her dad, so how can there be without him? She simply doesn't know how to live it, but somehow she is supposed to understand and figure it out without him? The thought of it creates insurmountable psychological chaos, and as she sits there in a defeated state, the preacher approaches her, kneels down and then answers her questions.

"You feel the hurt now. You will feel pain tomorrow, too, but the Lord will restore your soul. He will fill the void. That's how we stand here with you today," he continues, but Bailey suddenly looks up and into his eyes as he speaks because his voice completely changes. His voice sounds just like her father. "We've all lost someone, Bailey, but what we gain..."

"Daddy?" She stands from her seat before the crowd of onlookers, as the preacher continues to face forward, talking as if she's still sitting in front of him. "Why do you sound like my dad?" When the preacher continues talking to an empty seat, she then looks at her mother, who sits there listening to every word. "Mom! Mom! You don't hear him? He sounds like dad," she cries, upset and continuing to back away, and as she does, she bumps into Delight, but Delight is just like all the others, oblivious to her reality. Bailey touches her shoulder, but Delight doesn't feel anything. "Somebody!" she screams, but as she turns to face her dad's resting place, it's no longer there. Instead it's him. He standing there, watching her, and when he starts to talk, the preacher falls silent.

"Daddy? Is it really you, Dad," she weeps, confused but ever so grateful to see him again.

"Bailey," he calls as she attempts to reach for him. "No. You can't touch me, but yes, it's me. Don't come any closer to me. I have to give you something."

"But, Daddy..." she pleads, still moving toward him.

"Bailey, enough!" he orders so powerfully that the hair on her head moved with his breath, causing her to stop in her tracks, full of rage and disappointment.

"Why?!" she screams. "What did I do? Why are you doing this to me? You're my father!" she continues, believing that her dad is being cruel to her as she stands there grieving over him. She feels like she's a part of some cruel joke. "And what's wrong with everybody?" she shouts, but he puts his hand in the air in an attempt to signal her to calm down. She ignores him and instead, barrels toward him in a fit of rage as he attempts to stop her once more, however, his firm words are weak to her ears and determination. Therefore, he only stands there, and as she passes through him, his expression turns to misery because he can't physically comfort his own daughter.

"I'm no longer here, Bailey, but I'm not dead. I just can't stay long. Let me tell you what I need to tell you. There isn't much time," he continues facing away from her. As she stands behind him unable to console herself, he beckons her urgently once again. She finally faces his back. Then, he lifts his right arm, pointing directly a Delight. "Come see."

Bailey walks forward, and this time, she walks to his side. "Why are you pointing at Delight?"

"I didn't know that she was his daughter all this time, but you must destroy her, Bailey," he commands as he drops his eyes to admire his daughter face to face for one last time on the earth. "And you must destroy her before she kills you."

"What?" Bailey asks devastated, looking around at everyone surrounding his gravesite afraid that they heard what he said. "Dad, what are you talking about?"

"There is an explanation in your dreams. I kept it there to be shown only when you complete. I love you, Bailey. Obey me."

"Dad?"

Her father slowly disappears, and she's left with nothing but questions... and a crowd of people rushing to catch her before she plummets into the grave with her deceased father's casket.

## Black Fang | Chapter Eight

"Are you alright?" Delight asks, waiting outside of the bathroom as Bailey removes her funeral attire. When she gets no answer, she lightly knocks. "Bailey, I'm just checking on you. You can take as long as you want to change. The repass..."

"Go to the repass ahead of me, Delight. I can get there a little bit later." Bailey is extremely frustrated, battling between what has happened to her father and what is happening to her because of what her father said to her. She doesn't even know if it was real, but it seemed very real, atop the fact that she nearly fell over into the grave with him.

"What? No! I'm gonna take you back up."

"I'm not going back."

"Bailey, it's your dad's..."

Bailey bangs the door with her fist in such a rage that a slight crack enters into the frame but her hand feels absolutely no pain. "Don't talk about my dad!"

Delight isn't moved by Bailey's bang against the bathroom door. Instead, she's truly concerned about Bailey. "Bailey, listen. You passed out right there at his grave, like you literally walked over there and instead of stopping, you were about to go head first in before we stopped you. You don't remember that?"

"I told you in the car that *I don't remember*," she stresses. "I don't remember anything that you remember." She backs away from the bathroom door with an overwhelming sensation coming across her body that she's never felt before. All she knows is that she doesn't want Delight there while all these changes are going on. She doesn't want anyone there. She wants to be left alone so she can deal with what happened and why it occurred. "I must've blacked out, and I don't want to go back because I don't want people asking me questions, questions that I can't answer," she explains drifting off into her thoughts. Reaching over to the sink, she turns on the water. "You may as well go."

"Go?"

"Just go!" she exclaims, but her friend isn't just a friend but more like a sister.

"Bailey!" she shouts back, "My dad's been gone from my life, too. He's been gone for a while, and I know how much this hurts you. I know it does, but it was you who was there for me when I didn't know which way was up. Let me help you through this, Bailey, because you will get through it."

As Delight speaks, Bailey fights against the warning that she would have to destroy her best friend. It makes no sense, and all Bailey wants to do is fall asleep. Nothing makes sense yet, and somehow, her father told her that he tucked something inside her dreams, therefore, inside her dreams is where she wants to go.

Finally, there's silence, and it's during the silence that Bailey slides on a shirt and shorts that she has hanging on the towel bar, finally gathering the patience to open the bathroom door. There stands Delight against the hallway wall. She appears to be that same supportive friend that she's always been, except there's something tainted about her in Bailey's mind stemming directly from the death of her father.

"Delight?" Bailey fumbles, afraid of what she's about to reveal.

"What's up, Bailey? Whatever you have to say, just let it out. I know it's hard, but you'll get through it. You throw it, and I'll catch it, just like you did for…"

"Something's wrong with me. That's why I don't want to go back."

Delight approaches her slowly, believing that the ominous look on her face has to do with the horrible way in which her father passed away. However, as she dissects Bailey's appearance, she gets the deep feeling that there's more – much more. "This doesn't have anything to do with your father, does it?"

Bailey doesn't know what to say except, "Delight, it has everything to do with me … just me."

"I'm listening." Delight backs up and sits in the hallway, and seconds later, Bailey does the same, directly in front of her.

# Black Fang | Chapter Nine

"You gotta be kidding!"

"I'm not."

"Wait, let me do it."

"Are you serious?"

"Yes, move!" Delight said, shoving Bailey out of the way so that she could shove her head in the freezer for about five minutes. "You're sweating from being cold!"

"Yes, I need to stay away from extreme temperatures because I go in reverse," Bailey states, preferring to reveal her bodily temperature issues over what her dad told her.

"Did you tell your mom yet?"

"No, no," Bailey stresses. "I didn't tell her anything. I haven't had a chance, and I don't think I ever will, especially now. Something's different about me, and she is already dealing with everything," Bailey drifts off as Delight picks up.

"Well, my face is cold. There's no reverse affects happening on me." She moves away from the freezer and shuts the freezer door. "So how do you control it?"

"I don't. I haven't been in any extreme temperatures since the air conditioning unit got fixed. But you know what else?"

"What?"

"I'm starting to think all of this cold hot stuff has something to do with my dad."

"How do you mean?"

"I mean, this all started happening to me on the day that he died. Maybe it could be some sort of dimensional cross up, right?" Bailey suggests, hoping Delight has a definitive answer in some way.

"Never heard of it. Is that a thing?" Delight answers hesitantly.

Not wanting to tell Delight anything her father told her, she skates around the complete truth, turning her back to Delight and walking out of the kitchen into the dining area. "Well, yeah, like I heard somewhere that when some people pass away, sometimes they can leave stuff behind, like at the moment of passing."

"Like an animal sheds skin?"

"Sort of but not quite. I mean, what if I feel like this because it's somehow tied to my dad?"

Delight shuts the freezer and follows behind Bailey. "Well, if that's the case, then the dead really do talk."

Bailey spins around to face her. "What do you mean?"

"You're not the only one who had some kinda strange attack that day."

"You, too?"

Delight nods. They simultaneously sit at the kitchen table and silently wonder – what's going on? As Delight leans over placing her forehead on top of the table, Bailey stares at her as her father's words race through her memory. Was it real? Why would he want her to be afraid of Delight, so much so that he would order the most horrific thing? But what is it that he left inside her dream?

Suddenly, Delight breaks the silence. "The day your dad died, I cramped all up, too. I got really sick that day for a while but nothing too bad because it all went away. I think it was a dream though because I sorta passed out, tired. It was weird.

Maybe we're like sisters after all. Twins. I feel what you feel."

Bailey only stared back at her at a loss for words, briefly smiling and answering, "Yeah...that close."

# Black Fang | Chapter Ten

"I love you, Bailey. We're gonna get through this. We're gonna get through this together, all four of us, you, me, God and your dad. He's gonna always be with us, you hear me? Always." Bailey's mother kisses her on the cheek and wipes the tears from Bailey's eyes. Then, she pulls the sheets up and leaves Bailey's bedroom.

As soon as the bedroom light switches off, Bailey rests her eyes. Although she's thinking of her dad, she's nowhere close to dreaming. She's not even sleepy, and after lying there for one whole hour, there's still not an exhausted bone in her body. As a matter of fact, she hasn't been able to sleep since her dad died, and at the same time, she hasn't been as exhausted as she should be because sleep is something that she really hasn't gotten since the day he passed away.

"Come on, Bailey. Sleep," she commands herself as she flips onto her stomach, but after lying there for thirty more minutes, the sleep never comes down. Therefore, she sits straight up, turns on the light, and becomes filled with even more anxiety. "What is going on with me? Is this even real? When I need to go to sleep, I can't. Mom!" she calls.

"What?"

"May I come in there with you?"

"Yeah, baby. Bring your pillow."

"Thanks."

Bailey snatches her pillow from the bed, takes a deep breath, fighting against several strong emotions that have been boxing her since the death of her father and goes into her parents' bed. The light is off, but as she climbs onto the mattress, she hears her mother clearing her throat and sniffing her nose. They are both drained of everything, and nighttime is the worst part. Bailey is aware that it's especially hard on her mother at night because she used to share a bed with him. It even smells like him still which is odd. Her mom usually washes the sheets every week or at least changes them. However, this is the week that everything isn't the same. She changed nothing about the bedroom. The only thing that's different about the bed, the bedroom and the whole house is that the man of the house is no longer there, and he never will be again.

As Bailey lies there, her mom remains faced away from her. There's a pillow, her dad's pillow, that's leaning up against her back. Bailey can smell his scent in the covers, and she hesitates to lie down in his spot. She quakes with sadness, but forces back her tears so that her mother can grieve in peace without having to constantly console her. Suddenly, she changes her mind about sleeping in the bed with her mother. Instead, she kisses her on the cheek and leaves. Her mother doesn't move, and Bailey knows that it's her mother trying to remain strong. Therefore, she makes it easier for her to do so, and goes back into her bedroom, shuts the door and climbs back into her own bed. It takes her hours to get to sleep, but when she finally does drift off, she finds herself in a search, a search for the explanation of what her dad told her was tucked somewhere in her dreams.

Inside her dream, she's surrounded by darkness, even beneath her feet. When she walks, she's hesitant because she's walking on absolutely nothing at all, yet her feet are planting firmly on what feels like an invisible ground. Each step reveals footsteps behind her, and as she continues walking, oblivious of where she's going, she notices a faint shining object afar off that proves she isn't alone. It's a light, reminiscent of a star in the night sky. The only difference is that this glimmer of light is directly in front of her, not gleaming from above.

Bailey glances down again, and she understands now that she's walking on night. Night...it's solid, a different kind of night, not what she's learned before in school when they tell her it's simply the absence of light. This night is a substance, and she's walking on it. The darkness bounces from her feet like oil bounces atop water, gliding back down to connect with the darkness seamlessly as she makes her way toward the light that isn't increasing in size as she approaches. When she finally arrives, she looks around at the space, but it makes her feel lost, so lost that she is forced to concentrate on the only thing that centers her – the light.

The light is the size of the tip of her pinky, but it's bright. It stands out so much because of the darkness that surrounds it. It's extremely bright, but it's an oddity that the light isn't paining her eyes. As she stares directly into it, it does nothing. Therefore, she touches it. The light, then, engulfs her before expanding in all directions, revealing a place that she's never been, somewhere she's never imagined, but it feels so familiar. The place appears similar to earth, and maybe it is earth, just earth in another dimension. The grass is green but greener, and the sky is blue but a different shade of blue, like neon blue. Most everything is just like her side of earth except it's earth with a filter. As she admires the scenery, it's then that she recognizes her father.

"Dad?"

She calls, but he doesn't see her. In fact, more people are coming into focus, but she doesn't recognize any of them. They don't see her either. They walk right past her as if she isn't even there. She quickly turns to see what's behind her and everything is luminous, but no one sees her, though they see everyone else. Looking down, there's no longer a blank darkness beneath her feet but a flowing mirror with her reflection. She inspects the feet of everyone else, and notices that the mirror is just beneath hers. Finally, like the volume is turned up on a television, she hears the voices of everyone around her whispering, however, when her father begins to speak, the voices fall silent, just like the voices fell silent when he spoke at his funeral. She listens as he stands there speaking to someone on a sapphire street, appearing as if he is under some sort of assignment, like he's a general of some sort in a strange military.

Her father is draped in a black full body suit, black like jasper with traces of emerald green running through the black jasper as a stream down his sleeves and through his fingertips like overlapping veins. He appears much younger, and his physique is very muscular.

"Dad?" she calls him again, but he doesn't hear her. She finds the courage to step forward, but when she does, she's stopped by some invisible wall.

It's then that her father turns to look her square in the eye. His face is cold, and he's looks at her like he has no idea who she is. Then, he turns and walks away. At his disappearance, the scenery immediately changes, placing her inside a spacious room. The décor appears as if it's from the late nineteen eighties, early nineties. The television is like a big block, not a flat screen, and the telephone has a long cord as it hangs onto the wall.

As she looks around, she sees someone very familiar. It's her mom, but she's just as young as her dad who stands there looking normal, not like he did in the other dimension when he was wearing black and emerald. He just looks like a younger version of her dad. Bailey finally remembers where she is. She's in a picture! It's her parent's first apartment before she even existed! Then there's a knock on the door. Before going toward it, her dad looks at her again, and then, he opens the door.

Suddenly, Bailey no longer feels at home, but instead, there's the most intense feeling of mortality. The presence of it engulfs her. It feels like it's right behind her, and that's because it is. Bailey slowly turns around, and what is before her causes her to stumble and fall onto what has become concrete beneath her feet. Her father no longer looks like himself, but he's changed. Instead, he's the man in that black and emerald suit who has just murdered a man who she's seen before in cell phone pictures, a man who she's even heard stories about time and time again. That man is Delight's father, and he dangles by the hand of her own dad, staring wildly at her with a promise uttered directly at Bailey.

"She will avenge me," he promises before turning back to face her father, "And you know she will." Then, he smiles at both Bailey and her father before taking his last breath. It's then that her father drops him to the ground in horror, haunted by what the Delight's father just said. Blood drips from her dad's mouth as a huge gaping hole is revealed in the chest of Delight's father while he lies on the ground dead.

Bailey screams in terrible fright, running away from her own flesh and blood father. It's then that he appears directly in front of her, stopping her in her tracks. They're now surrounded by four walls that are only inches from their skin. Her father appears like his normal self once again, but Bailey's still sorely afraid. That's when he speaks.

"I didn't know that was Delight's father when I killed him. You two were not friends, and unfortunately, you're no longer friends anymore. He will influence her to kill you. Delight has no idea, or maybe she does know. I don't know but..."

"Kill me?"Bailey questions hysterically.

"Listen!" he pleads.

"Daddy..."

"Delight will see you as a never-ending, insatiable revenge soon, really soon. He will show her."

"Why did you kill him? Who are you?" she screams, "And how can he influence anything about her after his death? What are you talking about?"

He answers her by slamming his fist against the wall, causing each wall to crack, one after another. In a fury of frustration, he tries to get through to her again, "He is influencing her the same exact way that I'm influencing you, but he's not honest in doing so, but deceptive and skilled in that area! She will destroy you, Bailey! She will try and kill you, so that he can kill me in a sense for eternity… forever. You are my only offspring."

"I don't understand. Stop it!" Bailey shouts as the walls begin to crumble all around them. "Why did you kill him?"

"I had to, baby girl. I'm not totally who you think I am. I love you, Bailey. I love you and your mother. Go." He looks over to the side, beyond the crumbling walls, and it reveals her bedroom. They're now standing in it. "Everything will explain itself, and you will understand. Trust me. You must destroy her before she destroys you. Listen closely… protect your blood," he commands as he fades away.

"Daddy, don't leave me again. Come back," she calls as he disappears before her very eyes, leaving her all alone with a letter attached to the bedroom closet door. The walls around her are completely gone, and she's alone. Everything slowly becomes a shadow, while the letter shows itself brightly.  Bailey walks to it, and then she removes it from the closet door. It reads like a story, but the story is about her own family background, about a father whom she's now learning that she's really never known.

## Black Fang | Chapter Eleven

The Letter Reads...

"I'm not from earth in the same way that you are, Bailey, but I am as well, just in another dimension. No one from your side of earth has the power on their own to go or see where I'm from. I'm from a place called Tylon, and this makes me Tylonthian. The reason you've never met my parents is because they died in a war between us Tylonthians and a people that live amongst us of the same blood, but their belief system is totally different. They use their gifts for evil while we use ours to keep the peace. This is why we call them Lonthians. They've cut off their moral ties to Tylon and to their kin, us."

"A few of them, only a few, developed the power to escape Tylon over time without needing consent from the five elders over the five portals. There were particular, secretly communicated power sequences, and only the five elders held this power sequence on who could unlock and allow anyone to pass through to this side of earth, but somehow, that changed. The Lonthians are great workers of puzzles, and it was assumed that a few in particular had uncovered how the elders would work the code, but no one was certain if this was true at the time because use of the portals were not a usual thing. Whatever the case, them discovering the codes allowed for them to escape any form of attack from us Tylonthian heads, ordered by the elders. Delight's father was one of the ones who needed escape. Delight's father was a Lonthian assassin who would kill mainly Tylonthians despite the orders of the elders being to live in peace. I was given orders to stop him. He was one of the most dangerous because he was swift and cunning ... exceptionally smart. Upon his attack, Tylonthians would end up dead without a trace of evidence. It took much time and thought to determine it was him who was responsible for the deaths. When he knew I was onto him, he fled. He fled and hid in this side of earth for a long time which is why I ended up here as well. I searched high and low in Tylon for him, leaving my blood in places where he would frequent, but nothing. This is how I knew he was on this side ... without permission. They would have never let him leave because he has a thirst for death and to conquer. I have been long respected on this side, with a clean Tylonthian background. Therefore, at my request, I was allowed enter into here to find him and either bring him back or destroy him.

"The way you saw me as your father, that still is who I am, both on Tylon and in this Earth, except here, I changed to be and function more like a human being in order to live under the atmosphere, but my powers were still the same. The ability to die comes with that, though I was also able to die in Tylon, the death wasn't as imminent nor as easy. It actually doesn't happen fully. This is why you're reading this. I'll always have pockets of life and use them sparingly... and I will so that I can finish raising you."

"On my search for Delight's father here, I met and fell in love with your mother, and I was never supposed to fall in love or get married. Bailey, I loved her though, so much, and then you came, and

I knew then, I could never go back to Tylon. The longer I stayed on Earth, the weaker I would become because my body wasn't formed here, and I'd already shared my power … in you. This means that you will be more powerful here, where you were formed, than I ever could have been, even stronger than Delight's father, Xidon. This also means that Delight would have more power here as well."

"At my death, you automatically activated the inherited strength and life span of my own, but you also inherited the vengeance of Xidon. My real name is Yjotar. You are the daughter of Yjotar, Bailey. You have inherited certain powers from me that you have the ability to hide, but at times of defeat, death or defense, you will not be able to contain all of them. Therefore, be careful with every step, but when it's time, you must destroy Delight because she will no longer be your friend. She will be overcome by Xidon. His powers are great, but yours are greater. It is him you will have to destroy inside her. Keep this secret until it can be secret no more. Don't even tell your mother, and believe me, Bailey, I would never have put myself in the position to have taken his life if I would have known that he'd come into Earth and had a child ... never. In the position I was in...my powers... I had no option. The people here are in danger if you don't stop her. I never knew Delight belonged to him, never knew he even had a family. When she touched your blood the day I died, she also touched mine. That's when I knew that Xidon was still here and truly active in a descendant who was very close in proximity to you. Soon, you won't be friends anymore, Bailey. You will be enemies forever. Tylonthians and Lonthians are different, even genetically over the years. Remember that. Delight has been fully activated by our blood. She *is* activated to inherit all of Xidon now. Be very careful, Bailey. I'm sorry, Bailey. After this you can forever live your life. I will put nothing else on you. You have only one thing to do. I love you. Your father, Yjotar."

# Black Fang | Chapter Twelve

The Next Morning

"Bailey?" her mother calls slightly frightened, shaking her because she isn't waking up. "Bailey, baby?" She reaches over to shut the overpowering alarm clock off before leaning over to pat her daughter's face and feel for a pulse. "Bailey, come on, sweetheart, what's wrong? Wake up."

"Ma?" Bailey weakly utters finally.

"Oh, Lord Jesus, Bailey, you scared me. You weren't waking up," she exclaims, her hand clasping her chest as if she's about to pass out. Then, she sits on the edge of the bed, taking deep breaths, in an attempt to calm down. "I didn't know what was wrong with you. You've never done this before? Are you okay?"

"Ma, what's wrong?" Bailey asks, finally sitting erect on the bed, confused at her mother's posture.

"Bailey, you mean to tell me you really didn't hear me? I've been in here going on probably five minutes, and you wouldn't wake up. The alarm clock was going off, and you never shut it down, so I..."

"It went off?" Bailey peers at the clock then at the window. "It's already morning?"

"Yes, and unfortunately, I have to return to work and you to school. Listen, baby, I know it's been a couple of days, but you have to get your energy back. Yesterday, I let you sleep, and you barely ate..."

"I ate?" Bailey asks, pulling back the covers, confused on what her mom is talking about. She doesn't even recall yesterday happening.

"Bailey, are you okay? I know things have been rough, but we will make it. We have to. Now you *must* get to school today. You have no more days to miss."

"Missed school days? How long have I been asleep?"

"All night. What do you mean? You've been in the room for a couple days, but you've been up and about as normal. Don't tell me you don't remember being awake? Bailey, answer me."

"No...no ma'am. I don't remember. I just..."

"I'm calling a therapist right now."

"Wait, Ma... I'm just. Give me a minute. I'm tired that's it."

"No, no...I'm calling. Do you even know what day it is?"

"Tuesday. Mom, it's Tuesday," she guesses, and is shocked she's right. "I know what's going on, Ma. I was just in a deep sleep. I didn't sleep for days after Daddy died."

Her mom moves from the bed, and then leans over to kiss Bailey's forehead, resting her cheek atop Bailey's face. "I know you're exhausted. I lay in bed all week thinking of him, and once I even thought he was really in the bed with me. My body feels drained, and I know yours does as well, but we're strong. God says be strong, and if He says it, He will give us strength. Love you. Shoot me a text when you get to school or do you need me to take you there? You can't miss..."

"I know, Ma. I can't miss, but wait...I know you hate when I ask, but may I please make some coffee?"

"I have never believed that coffee is a teenage drink, Bailey. Call me old fashioned, but to me, it's for older folks like me, or at least people who work full-time, who have no energy left," she laughs. "That's why I don't want you drinking any like I do. I have a purpose for my caffeinated coffee. Your body already makes natural caffeine around the clock."

Bailey smiles and jokingly rolls her eyes, "Please, Ma. I think I feel like you today."

"Well," she continues, leaning in to kiss her daughter on the forehead, "you can drink what I leave for you. I'm about to take mine on the road." She starts to leave the room, but hesitates, "And, baby, you call me – for anything. No more rules. You can call me just to say hello. I'll stop work, okay?"

"Alright. Love you, Ma."

"Love you more. I mean what I said," she stresses as she walks from the bedroom and into the kitchen where Bailey listens to her prepare her coffee before leaving the house. When the door closes, Bailey jumps up from the bed and rushes in front of her mirror.

"Why don't I remember anything? What's going on with me?" She yanks the skin on her face and pinches herself to make certain she isn't in a dream because the dream is the only thing she remembers. Going to bed a couple days ago is the last thing she remembers after crawling from her mother's bed. Then...

"I got stuck in the dream for days?! This can't be right. Something is way off. I couldn't have been awake and asleep at the same time. No way!" she says, rushing to her cell phone. She and Delight normally text each other every single day, so she pulls up her messages, and there they are, a full two days of messages – detailed messages – about how she missed out on what happened in school, who broke up with whom, and even how she would drop her school assignments off during her time of bereavement.

"Assignments?"

Bailey searches her room for any evidence of assignments but none are there, and then, she finally peeps inside her book bag. Removing all the folders, she then sees a whole new assignment, and it's complete! She drops the completed assignment back into her book bag, stunned.

"No way. There's no way." She runs to the kitchen and searches through the refrigerator. "What did we eat last night? I can't even remember," she panics, but then she settles down when she finds a pot full of spaghetti and meatballs. She then looks in the dishwasher. "Two plates! I actually ate?"

Although flabbergasted, she snaps out of it, leaves the kitchen to get ready for school, and before she leaves the house, she downs the coffee her mom left. "I can't believe this," she whispers, fumbling at the front door with the keys in order to lock the door. "I cannot believe this *at* all. *At all*!"

Suddenly, a car beeps its horn, and Bailey leaps from her skin as she looks back to see who it is. It's one of her dad's friends that she'd noticed at the funeral, hugging everyone and paying respects.

"Hey there! I tried to catch your mother. Tell her I stopped by. Name's James. Your father was a good man, and I just want to let y'all know that my family and my home is available for you whenever. Just call. If you need any money or anything, just holler. Your mom knows me and my wife. James. James and Tammy Walker. I'm just passing by. I'm gonna sure miss your daddy. Let your mom know that I'll handle the yard work twice a month for free."

"Okay, Mr. Walker. Thank you," she responds putting her book bag on her shoulder, "I'll tell her." She waves as she eyes the lawn equipment on the trailer of his truck, figuring he must own his own lawn care business.

"You take care now. Get to school safe."

Bailey waves her hand, and when he leaves from her home, she heads on to school, scrolling through her phone to catch up on all the conversations she somehow doesn't remember, but then she suddenly pauses, becoming extremely anxious, causing her nerves to shatter.

"Calm down, Bailey, calm down," she says, soothing her anxiety only for a brief second before her cell phone rings. She discovers it's Delight and breathes a sigh of relief, answering, "Hey, Delight."

"Hey, friend. Are you on your way to school again? You good?"

"As good as I can be I suppose. I'm having a hard time remembering certain things."

"Certain things like what? Oh...remember what you said yesterday about the football coach? You were right!"

"I was?" Bailey answers completely clueless, placing Delight on speaker phone so that she can run through her messages once more to find out what's going on with the coach.

"Were you? He's outta there. Gone."

"Good?"

"Good?" Delight questions. "No, bad. Bad, bad, bad. Remember, he was set up. Completely lied on?"

"Oh yeah..."

"You hit the nail on the head. How did you even know that?"

"Gut?"

"That's impossible. How would you have even known this was gonna happen? You weren't even in school!"

"Hey, Delight?" Bailey asks, frustrated and ready to end the call.

"What's up?"

"I need to check something out. I'll see you in class okay?"

"You alright?"

"Yeah, I'm good. See you at the lockers."

"No, don't hang up!"

"What?" Bailey snaps, but quickly apologizes.

"It's normal. Forgetfulness. It happened to me when my dad died. With me, it was random. I understand. Sometimes, I would forget to even eat..."

"It's not like that," Bailey responds as she jogs to the bus stop as the bus makes its stop at the edge of the road. "I don't remember anything. Not even what I told you about the coach."

"You mean you don't remember anything?"

"Nothing."

Feeling completely lost inside her own body, Bailey ends the call without a good-bye and steps onto the school bus. Everyone, including the bus driver, greets her warmly, and when she gets to her regular seat, she sees a multitude of flowers and sympathy cards. She thanks everyone, sits down and holds in her cry throughout the ride, pretending that all is fine, when in reality, it isn't anywhere close.

`

Upon arrival at school, Bailey exits the bus, leaving her items on the school bus, and moseys to her locker where Delight stands with a breakfast sandwich in hand and a small soda.

"Brought you some! I already ate mine. Mom dropped me off this morning early, so we decided to grab you something. Bailey? You good?" she asks, puzzled at why Bailey stands about ten feet from her without walking forward or reaching for the warm breakfast. "Bailey," she continues, walking forward to shake her shoulder in order to somehow snap her from her daze. When she does, Bailey jerks away from her hand, almost involuntarily. Not only does Delight notice, but Bailey is very aware of what just happened.

"I hurt my shoulder," Bailey lies, throwing her hand up to fake the protection of her shoulder. She's on edge about not only her father's death, but everything that has taken place since, including his message about Delight. A sense of gloom hovers over her now that she's in front of Delight, and she can't shake it. "Thanks for the breakfast. I was just standing back here for a second, wondering if I should go back home. I don't know if I want to be here."

Realizing everything is off, Delight moves back and asks, "What happened to your shoulder?"

"I fell ... fell into the side of the doorway. Tripped up and boom."

"Boom, huh?"

Bailey politely takes the breakfast and walks around Delight while answering, trying to avoid eye contact, "Boom. The bruise is gone down though."

"That fast?"

"Yeah, just that fast."

"You're right handed, Bailey. You're carrying your book bag on that same right shoulder that's supposed to be super sore from a fall."

Bailey stops turning the combination at her locker and closes her eyes in order to concentrate on keeping her father's secret message from her mind, but no matter how hard she concentrates, the darkness behind her eyelids reminds her. Therefore, she opens her eyes again, puts her forehead against the locker and apologizes.

"I'm sorry, Delight."

"Listen," she responds, "I'm not even mad at you because I've been where you..."

"But aren't you?" Bailey retorts, rudely interrupting Delight, taking her by surprise at the tone. "Aren't you angry at me for something?"

"Am I what? Bailey, what's..."

"Nothing." Bailey proceeds to unlock her locker as Delight stands there dumbfounded. "Delight, I'm just," she begins to explain as she opens her locker, but as she does, Delight touches her arm in an attempt to connect with her best friend in mourning. However, the connection unleashes something that the both of them feel, and immediately, they disconnect. Bailey stares back at Delight and notices the disdain and depletion in Delight's eyes, and she knows something is horribly wrong.

"Delight?"

Instead of answering, Delight continues to stare her in the face, directly into her eyes, and slowly walks away as tears fill her eyes. Then, out of nowhere, Delight whispers, "Stop it. Stop, Bailey. Stop..." she continues, her voice raising, until she speaks her last words before the bell rings for class, "Close your eyes!"

Quickly, Bailey closes them, fearing the worst, and the worst is what happened. When her eyelids meet, she captures what Delight probably saw – her father being killed. "Delight!" she shouts, opening her eyes only to discover that the hallway is empty, and she's late for class.

# Black Fang | Chapter Thirteen

"Have a seat, Bailey. It's good to have you back. Do you have a..."

"No. No, ma'am, I don't. I'm just tardy," Bailey answers with her head down as she walks to her seat. The teacher stands there uneasy about being hard on her about tardiness due to it being her first day back since her father passed away, so she dismisses the discipline and returns to teaching.

Bailey places her bag on the floor, removes her assignments and walks over to place them in the due basket before returning to her seat. When she sits back down, there's already a note on her desk. She flips the top of the folded paper, and it reads, "I'm sorry about everything. I texted you, but you never returned my texts. I didn't text you anymore, but that doesn't mean I wasn't thinking about you every day. Just wanted to give you space."

She looks up from the note, and despite the fact that it has no name on it. She knows exactly who it's from. When she glances over his way, he isn't looking back at her. Instead, he's busy writing whatever the teacher has written on the white board. Therefore, she does the same, deciding to talk to him later instead of sending a note back.

His name is Eric, and he's been the closest guy in her life since middle school. They don't hang out all the time, but when they do, it's always different, different than any other conversation she's ever had with anyone else. There are days when Bailey even prefers his company, but she's never told him that. He's a calm guy, almost like nothing ever bothers him or gets him out of his element. Besides being extremely smart, making all school work look overly simple, he's caring, beyond words.

When class ends, she rushes over to him as he heads for the door. "You're walking out of class like you don't want a response."

He turns back with a smile. "I knew you would respond sooner or later. You know I don't press you for anything. I'm not even like that. You alright?"

"You know what, Eric? I don't think so."

Eric not only senses but sees clearly that she needs more than just small talk, so he takes her by the hand and says, "Are you okay to come with me?"

"Where?"

"I uh... I think we need to skip our next class. We're not going off the campus or anything like that."

"Where though if not off campus?"

"Just to talk. You need it. Nobody walks on third wing at this time. You know they have that renovation going on back there. We don't have to go if you don't want to go, but by the way those tears look like they want to fall out of those dark brown eyes..."

Bailey looks down and away from him. "Yeah, I need to... at least to get myself together."

"Cool. Wait a second for me right here in the hall. I'll be right back, alright?"

She nods her head, still feeling so lost, confused about not being able to remember absolutely anything except for the worst parts about her life for the last days – her father's death and her dream that came with the dreaded message from her father about Delight and Delight's father. How is she ever going to be able to...

"You ready?"

"Yeah," she responds to Eric as he keeps his word, coming right back.

"I got us something even better."

"Like?"

"Two passes to the library."

"The libary?"

"Yeah."

"How?"

"Easy. That's my family."

"Are you serious?"

"Yeah. He normally doesn't pay me any attention, but since he knows I'm serious about you...uh your situation...he knows it's empty, and you need some space. I just got you that space and a reason to be out of class. Do a little research," he smiles.

"Research," Bailey repeats, smiling back and rolling her eyes.

"Yeah, on each other."

Bailey hears him, but she doesn't respond because she always clams up whenever he flirts with her and today is no different. Sometimes, she can't gage him because even when she thinks he's playing around, he's also so sincere at the same time.

The library is quiet as it should be. Eric seems to know exactly what to do, like he's done this plenty times before with fake passes, and Bailey follows, believing that he has everything covered.

There's a spot at the very back of the library where they choose to sit, and right before they sit down, Eric randomly grabs two of the biggest books he could find and places them both on the table.

"For us," he says as we both sit down. "Let's open them up and chat."

Bailey can only laugh as he adjusts his seat beside her, opens his book and completely ignores it, giving all his attention to her. It makes her feel good, really special. She also opens her book and turns toward him. "Thanks. Do you do this often?"

"No problem. I got you. No, not often. Time after time. Sometimes, I need to be alone. Can't do it too much or I will get caught. Three times a year or so, and this is one of those times. You're in a rough spot, Bailey. You can't just go about life like normal right now because everything isn't normal. It's the craziest thing ever to be expected to do that in a couple days. I get it."

"Have you ever lost someone?"

"Me? Nah. Never. Not like you have. I've tried to hold on to some people though. That was hard enough, so I can only imagine. But this isn't about me. What's on your mind? I'm listening."

Bailey goes quiet, and all Eric does is wait. He reads her well, and he always has. Finally, she takes a deep breath and begins, "I can trust you right?"

He nods.

"I don't think I'm okay. I mean, I'm here with you, and I look fine, but I'm not fine on the inside. The reason I'm not okay is because sure, my father has died, but there's more. He's not really gone, Eric."

Eric doesn't say anything. He only touches her hand, bringing her enough comfort and strength to continue. She momentarily takes her attention to the gentle caress of his fingers across hers before she speaks again.

"I know this is gonna sound crazy, but I'm not crazy. My father..." she says as the tears start flowing at the mention of him, "he spoke to me face to face at the funeral, right before he was buried, and he told me something about Delight." She waits on him to start laughing or bolting from the library, but he doesn't. As she continues to stare down at the awful library carpet, he leans over closer to her.

"Go ahead, Bailey, speak your mind. I'm good on everything you're saying. No need to be ashamed."

She doesn't flinch at his words because she's trying to find the words to tell him what her father told her about Delight and how she has to somehow destroy her. As she sits there in limbo for about two minutes silently, she finally gives up, snatches her hand away from his, and stands to leave. However, she's stopped, not by force but by words.

"Bailey," Eric calls still seated. "I'm from Tylon."

"What?" She spins around stunned. "What did you just say?"

# Black Fang | Chapter Fourteen

"Adopted?" Bailey asks, still in shock that Eric even knows of this place she'd never even been to called Tylon. "So you mean that..."

"Yeah, calm down," he whispers as he looks around cautiously. "We're still in the library, you know, the place where no one should hear us."

"But..."

"Like I said, I'm sort of adopted. My family, the same family member that gave me these passes to the library, is my sort of adoptive family," he continues, drifting off deep in thought before getting those thoughts back on track, "who let me live with them. I went with them when I left Tylon as a child, that would be ten years old here."

"Here? What do you mean here? So you're a different age over there in Tylon?" she asks, waving her hand to the side like she can reach into the Tylon dimension.

"You can put your hand down," he smiles. "I was twenty in Tylon years, but it equates to here as ten. Every year, we are double. I wasn't ready to adhere to the rules, or the rite of passage. There, it's mandatory, so I left."

"Well, I thought people couldn't just leave?"

"Can't. Most can't. I waited until I memorized how they did it. That's when I did it, too."

"The Lonthians?"

"Your dad told you a lot. Tylonthians... we are mostly adherers to rules and tradition, daring not go against it. Lonthians are different. I sorta took their lead on this one, just to get out of Tylon. I'm sure may Tylonthians know the code, but they want to stay. Tylonthians are generally very loyal while Lonthians function more by whatever works in their favor. It's the one thing I don't regret though...leaving." He leans back in the chair with his hands behind his head, inhales, and then leans in close, taking both her hands into his own. "I've always known who you are since I first spoke to you, since I first saw you. I'd just never met a half human, half Tylonthian before."

"So you knew about this, about me and my dad all along?"

"I knew about you because I saw your dad. Now, since his death, I know you've changed over. I knew I couldn't ever let him see me because he would know. Sometimes, I think he would sense my being around, but he never saw me. He's okay by the way."

"My dad?"

"Yeah. We don't die really. Us...me, you, everyone..."

"What do you mean?" she asks as he stands from his chair and stretches.

"We don't die. We just go missing until we see each other again. That's all. That's what I did when I left. I just went missing from there, and now I'm here. When I actually die, I'm still here, just there somewhere."

"And your parents?"

"They're fine. They know I'm just somewhere else. If something terminal happens to me, they will know immediately."

"That's wild. Are you ever going back?"

He sits back down, leans forward and places his head on the table. "I was going to...someday."

"Was?"

"You're in trouble." He lifts his head, staring forward before glancing to the side at Bailey. "I can't leave you here alone like that. That wouldn't be Tylonthian of me." He reaches over and holds her hand. "I noticed a change in the atmosphere here in the school. Your dad was right. You're in danger, sooner than later."

"Well, what do I do?" Bailey stresses. "I'm not gonna kill anyone, not Delight, not *anyone*."

"Don't worry. You won't until you have to. It was a part of your father's gift. In Tylon, he could never get in trouble because his gift was purely on self defense. This is why he was chosen for what would be known here as police work. He makes no mistakes."

"I don't understand."

"He can't kill, not voluntarily.  It's hard to explain, but what he does isn't murder. It's not involuntary either. It's a hormone that releases in his system only when death is necessary. Like in science when white blood cells only multiply more when someone is sick. You can't control it. It just happens as a defense to save the body."

"You talk about my father like he's still here, in the present."

"To me, he is."

"So he doesn't try to terminate anyone, but it just happens?"

"Yes…" he stumbles, "As a result of energy. Whenever his life is in danger from another, he can feel the exact moment he will be destroyed. There's something like a hormone that takes over and he defends himself without regard for life. It's not fear that causes it. Fear won't bring about lethal self defense. It's like is body knows, like he sees it ahead of time."

"You said this was my father's special gift."

"Yeah."

"Everyone has different gifts?"

"Yeah, like people here. Your dad is well known in Tylon."

"So you think that same gift he had…"

"Yeah, he wouldn't have told you to carry out a mission if you didn't have it." He looks up at the clock. "We need to get out of here. Are you sure you're okay?"

"Confused but okay. What do I do about Delight though?"

"Nothing, until you have to do something."

At that, they leave the library.

# Black Fang | Chapter Fifteen

The lunch bell rings, and Bailey is finally able to escape class, a class that felt like torture because inside the class along with her, right beside her, sat Delight. The tension throughout the class was worse than any tension they'd ever had from any stupid argument or disagreement. This tension couldn't even be cut with a knife. It had to be chopped with an axe, and neither one of them was willing to pick it up and cut.

As Bailey steps outside the classroom, she feels all the eyes landing on her and Delight's odd behavior toward one another. Delight won't look at Bailey, and Bailey only cut her eyes at Delight, trying to determine exactly what to do next, if anything at all. To Bailey, everything is so messed up, and all she wants is for everything to go back to the way they used to be.

"Bailey."

"Yeah?" It's Delight. Bailey drops her pen on the floor as she turns to face her, but doesn't dare look her in the eyes because of what she believes happened the last time.

"So are we doing lunch in the canteen or the lunchroom?"

"Lunch?" Bailey asks picking up her pen from the floor, completely not understanding what's going on.

"I probably over reacted earlier. You did just lose someone..."

"I lost my *dad*," Bailey responds, slightly irritated by how Delight calls him *someone* as if he was just an associate, but instead of erupting, she remembers about Delight's father. Therefore, she holds her contempt back.

"Yeah, you lost your dad," Delight continues unbothered and unmoved by how Bailey snapped back at her. Her face was expressionless, but the tone of her voice carried all expression of care and concern as she continued speaking. "I was about to say someone who was closest to you...before you cut me off."

"Oh...sorry for..." Bailey responds, guilty and ashamed of how she's been behaving toward her.

Then she finally decides to look Delight in her face and blurt everything out that's going on. "Delight, I need to tell you…"

"Don't worry about it. Let's go," Delight shrugs it off as she starts to walk with Bailey to her locker, and that's when Bailey spots Eric in the distance, shaking his head, barely enough for her to notice the motion. Instead of answering him back with any action, she simply slams her locker and turns to walk with Delight. They decide to eat in the lunchroom instead of the canteen.

"It'll be the lunchroom today. They're having my favorite."

"They are, aren't they?"

"Yeah," Bailey lightly smiles, glancing over her shoulder to see if Eric is still there before turning the corner. He is, but she can see the worry in his face. Despite that, she continues around the corner and down the corridor until reaching the lunchroom. Strangely enough, after entering the lunchroom and getting their trays of food, as they both walk to a lunchroom table, there's Eric sitting down already with a bag lunch waving her over.

Bailey gladly accepts though uncertain on how he beat them to the lunchroom.

"Hey, Delight? Let's go sit with Eric today."

"Sure."

"Sure?"

"Yeah," she smiles. "What?" she continues, questioning why Bailey is so shocked at her response.

"No argument about sitting with Eric?"

"No. Why would I have a problem with sitting with Eric?"

"Because sometimes you do, that's why," Bailey reminds her.

"Not today," she continues, walking towards the table as Eric sits there waiting on a wise crack from Delight.

"What's up, Delight? You got something for me today?" he asks with his whole guard up.

"No, no jokes today. I'm just trying to be here for Bailey. She's been through a lot, and whatever she needs, even if it's sitting at a table with *an Eric*, she can have."

111

"I think *an Eric* counts as a wise crack," Bailey inserts as Eric grins and continues with his lunch, behaving as if he knows nothing about the situation between Bailey and Delight. The lunchroom is packed, and the more packed it gets, the louder it becomes. It just so happens, the loudest group of teens is seated directly behind Bailey, so she raises her voice to break what has become an unusual silence between the three of them. "I know my dad has passed away, you guys, but try and be normal during lunch. Like right now, Eric, how about toss me some of that chocolate candy. Bet you five dollars I won't miss," she smiles as Eric tosses the first one. She catches it but knocks over her drink.

"Oh shoot!" Bailey shouts as she catches her balance, but when she looks onto the cafeteria floor, there's no spill. Not only was there no spill, but there was also no soda on the table either. "Where's my..."

As she focuses her attention on Eric, she quickly notices that his attention is elsewhere, and when she looks at Delight, all her confusion becomes as clear as a crystal. There's Delight, holding her soda from the top and she's staring directly into Eric's eyes. Both their faces are stern, like two boxers about to go through round one of a boxing match, and Bailey sits there like a horrible referee.

"Delight? Eric?" Bailey prompts, and when she does, Delight simply places her soda back on the table without flinching her focus away from Eric. It's then that Eric finally relaxes his posture, picks up his sandwich and slowly shifts his eyes away from Delight.

"You knocked your drink over," Eric alerts her seconds later.

"Yeah, I see that," she responds, cutting her eyes to the side as Delight removes her hand from the drink, finally taking her attention off of Eric. "Thanks, Delight."

"No problem. You gotta watch yourself, sis. Accidents happen *all* the time, and I can't be here *all* the time to save you…" she states solemnly before releasing a huge burst of laughter, "with all my skills! You should have seen Eric's face when I caught it. The fastest thing he'd ever seen, huh, Eric?"

Eric bounces his eyes toward Bailey before getting up from his seat. "Yeah, uh, it was fast. Never seen anything quite like it...on earth. Listen, Bailey, I'll talk to you later, alright, about that assignment we're paired up to do from class," he lies, throwing Bailey off guard for a couple of seconds before she catches on.

"Yeah, okay. Call me after school."

"I might even stop by because I'll be in the area." He looks back at Delight and exits. "See ya, Delight."

"Don't we always see each other?"

"Delight! Chill."

"I am chill. Very." She smiles at Bailey and then turns to finish her lunch as Bailey watches Eric walk away.

"Thank you! I appreciate you so much," she says, as the students from the school bus place her flowers and gifts at her doorstep before rushing back to the school bus. School is out and even though she has a pile of homework, homework is the furthest thing from her mind.

Grappling with all the gifts as well as everything that went on in school earlier, she carefully places all the items onto the sofa and heads to the bathroom to wash her hands before getting something to eat. As she sits her cell phone on the dining room table, she makes certain the volume is turned all the way up and that it's connected to the charger. Eric looked like he'd seen a ghost with white sheets and all in the lunchroom, and she didn't know what she missed between catching food in her mouth and knocking over her drink. It all happened so fast. She barely finished her food at lunchtime, and now, she's desperately hungry without a memory of what is in the fridge from even a day ago. Therefore, she searches the kitchen.

"Yes!" she exclaims, relieved. "I have a salad tucked back here, and if it's not mine, it is now," she shrugs as she removes it from the fridge and goes over to finish reading the sympathy cards given to her from her schoolmates. "Mom is going to flip when she sees all this," she says to herself as she crunches down on some lettuce and cucumbers. Opening one of the cards guides her emotions into such gratefulness, and thoughts of her father overtake her so much until tears come to her eyes...before a very loud knock rattles her from her thoughts.

She drops her fork, terrified at the erratic knocking, and heads over to the peephole. Then, she swings the door open, "Eric? What are you doing here? Wait...I forgot you said you were coming over."

"I...I...I...uh...you need to listen to your father as soon as possible," he orders, barging his way into the home frantically, glancing at all the sympathy cards before refocusing.

"Well, come on in. Have a seat. Fix a burger...which I don't have," she says sarcastically while shutting the door behind him.

"Listen, Bailey," he fumbles out of breath, "I ran all the way here because I have to tell you up front. You are *definitely* in trouble. Never be alone with Delight – ever. If you are, then you will have to..."

"Wait. Slow down. What's going on? You went from calm about the situation earlier, and now you're freaking me completely out. Since when is it so..."

"Real? It's real," he says, grabbing her hand and tugging her over to the sofa.

"Wait! Don't sit on my gifts," she panics as he maneuvers elsewhere before she takes his hand and shifts him to the floor with her. She sits cross-legged, and he kneels, speaking to her as directly as he can.

"Bailey, you missed it. It happened just that fast. I know who her dad is, and it's worse than what I thought."

"What?"

"Either you and your mom have to leave or..."

"What do you mean?"

"You know how I'm talking to you, and you're you?"

"Yeah?"

117

"Well, I don't think she's herself, especially when around you. I think she is who she is everywhere else, but whenever she gets around you, he worsens."

"He who?"

"Her father."

At his words, Bailey slouches. "My dad told me about her father... the Tylon version."

"Yes, but just listen. Here's one of her strengths, she's super fast. Watch this." He stands up and moves from one part of the room to another. "You saw me right?"

"What the...?" she responds stunned.

"Well, you actually *saw* me. You can't see her."

"Is that how you beat me to the lunchroom?"

"Bailey, snap out of it. I'm serious, and yes, that's how I beat you to the lunchroom. I move pretty fast when no one is looking just to save time. Anyway..."

"Can I do it?"

"Probably but everyone moves at their own speeds, but, Delight, her father is the fastest. I didn't see her move. She just suddenly had your drink in her hand. Before I even left, there were stories about the fastest one in Tylon. It really is her father. It must be."

"You mean she's possessed?"

"Something like that. If she's not possessed, she's exactly as fast as her dad, maybe faster, but if she is, you need to practice."

"I do?"

"Yeah, you do," he says nodding his head. "Stand up. I need you to grab me, okay?"

"Grab you." She reaches over to hold his arm. "Okay, now what?"

He removes her arm and looks up toward the ceiling frustrated. "I mean to try and grab me when I start moving. I'm going to move as fast as I can, and I need you to practice not only seeing everything I'm doing, but I need you to remember what I did. At the same time, I need you to grab me. Understand?"

"Will I even be able to do it if I'm not fast enough?"

"That's the thing," he sighs, gently grabbing her hands, lifting them into his. "No, Bailey, you won't be able to if you aren't fast enough. I just need to see if you can, to put myself at ease, so please, I need you to concentrate. Will you do that for me?"

Bailey slides her hands from his when she senses just how serious he is. "Yeah, yeah." She then steps back. "Go ahead. Start," she says taking a deep breath before concentrating. Before she notices, he's already gone. At first, she doesn't see him, but within seconds, she's on him with her eyes, monitoring everything he's doing. He's doing the same thing over and over again, and she's memorizing his every move. When she has it memorized, she leans forward, bracing herself to try and grab him, but each time she tries, she fails. No matter how much she sees him, she's not able to grab him, and after so many attempts, she gives up.

"Stop! Just stop! What if I can't grab you? What does this mean for me, Eric? Huh? What does it mean?"

Eric stops directly in front of her distress and answers, "It means you might not make it, Bailey." His words cause a silence, but he refuses to waste time or deliver anymore doubt. "Tell me, what new have you discovered about yourself since the passing of your dad?"

"Well, I know I can't remember anything much from last week, and...and when it gets too hot, I get super cold. When it gets too cold, I get super hot. And then there's the extra teeth."

"Extra teeth? You have some extra teeth?" he states excited, trying to see inside her mouth.

"Yeah, I have fangs," she responds awkwardly. "I would show them to you, but I can't make them come back out."

"Those are your main defense. They won't come out. What else?"

"My main defense?"

"Bailey, what else?" he urges, desiring to move beyond her new fangs.

"I uh...I felt Delight. I could feel her when she touched my blood."

"You sure you could actually feel her?"

"Yes, yes, I know I could, and when I felt her, I remember knowing something was different about her. I just didn't know fully because there's also something different about me. You know how you say she isn't always the same Delight, well, sometimes, I'm not the same me. This is all so new, Eric," she stresses.

"No, no. This is good. What needs to happen is that you develop at the same rate she develops or faster." He places his hands on her shoulders. "Think of every way your gifts benefit you in any battle."

"Battle?"

"Yes. Your fangs, I already can tell you that they are your terminators. There's no coming back after those come out. You won't be able to make them come down unless you are about to be killed."

"That's what I can't control...the thing you said were like hormonal."

"Yeah. It's a common gift for those like your father. I still can't believe you inherited it. But think about your hot and cold. You need to find out how to defend yourself and fight in both temperatures. Your skills will probably change, so you need to understand your body."

"You really think this battle between me and Delight will happen, don't you?"

"I don't think. I know."

As they continue to practice, Delight stands across the street on the sidewalk watching through the sheer curtains that are pulled ever so slightly open.  She stands in awe at how amazing Bailey moves as well as Eric, still amazed that he is from Tylon just like her father. As she studies them both, she feels a small beat of rage enter her heart. It enters from the right side and circles round and round like its own solar system. The more the rage, the faster it revolves, and the better Delight feels. She feels so powerful that she can move the air, so she does. As she inhales a deep refreshing breath, she erupts in giggles as she watches the oxygen molecules enter her nose, leaving a huge area absent of gases that are necessary for life. A small puppy with its owner passes by as Delight takes another deeper breath, controlling everything she inhales. When the owner with pup walks directly in front of Delight, the puppy whimpers, trying to rush forward while the owner stops, seemingly choking, not able to get any air in. Quickly, Delight flinches from her deep breath when she notices the woman choking and releasing the leash, allowing her puppy to run off terrified.

"Ma'am, ma'am?"

"I can't breathe! Something's wrong. Please," she begs as her eyes begin straining and the veins in her neck protrude. As seconds go by, she can no longer talk, but as Delight rushes to move her over into the grass, immediately, the woman inhales and can breathe as if nothing was wrong.

"Oh my goodness!" the woman exclaims while inhaling heavily in an attempt to rescue herself from passing out. "I don't know what happened! Oh thank you so much. Thank you!" Then, she looks up in search of her puppy who has already slowed to a stop at the end of the street, whimpering fearfully. She calls him, and the pup hesitantly returns. "I'm going straight to the hospital. Thank you so much. I don't know what's wrong with me," she continues as she walks off toward her puppy, whipping out her cell phone to call someone whom she talks to a mile a minute. Meanwhile, Delight ponders what just happened, and just as she links it together, Mrs. Conyers steps outside her front door, staring directly at Delight standing on her grass.

"Young lady, may I help you?"

Delight jumps, "Ma'am?"

"Don't I know you?"

"No," Delight answers, hiding her face and running off. "No, I'm sorry for walking across your property."

"I do know you!" Mrs. Conyers shouts after her before quieting down and going back inside her house. "I sure do know her. That's Bailey's little friend." The screen door slams behind her, and seconds later, she's peering curiously through her window again.

# Black Fang | Chapter Sixteen

"Wait," Eric abruptly says looking out of the window. "You didn't see that?"

"See what?" Bailey answers as she focuses on how her body moves in front of a space heater. A portion of her body is getting colder than the other side that isn't up against the heater, so she's comparing the differences of motion and strength as Eric advised her to do.

"I could have sworn I saw someone outside across the street who looked just like Delight. Maybe it was Delight."

"Are you serious?" Bailey asks, halting her practice.

"Yeah," he mumbles while peeking through the sheer curtains before moving them all the way back. "Were you expecting her?"

"No...uh...no," she replies, glancing down at her cell phone. "She didn't tell me she was coming over. Are you sure it was her?"

"Wasn't she wearing a pink and white shirt today with some cut up blue jeans and those pink sneakers?"

"Yeah."

"Well, that's why I think that was her. She took off down the road." He turns to face Bailey with a grim countenance. "I think she was watching us, mainly you, but she saw me, too."

"What does that mean?"

"It means I could be in danger, too."

"Oh crap." She flops down on the couch, completely stressed and at a loss on what's next. "Are you hungry?"

"A little bit."

"Good. Let's go."

"Go where?"

"With me." She sends her mom a text message that she will be out and will be home soon. Then, she slides her cell phone in her pocket, and they both head out the door.

"Bailey, you can't be serious. Stop playin'," he states, noticing they're in route to Delight's house.

"Oh yes I am serious."

"What's the purpose?"

"To ask her why she walked all the way over here to look into my window."

"You can't call her on the phone?"

Bailey stops on the sidewalk and faces Eric before asking, "Couldn't she have called me or knocked on my door instead of staring in my window like a creep?" Then she starts walking again, leaving Eric behind pondering how tragic going to Delight's house could become.

"Well, you have a point. Still yet..." he says catching up to her in an attempt to calm her down as she is getting more upset with each step.

"There is no *still yet*, Eric. Despite all that's going on, she is still my best friend, and I love her like a sister. I mean, am I supposed to just do as my father says, and what you say, just because you said it? What if there's another way? What if I can tell her, talk to her, have her understand what's going on if she doesn't already and then we can both shut this all down? Isn't that a more perfect plan than some slay theory, from a place I've never been by the way, called Tylon? Is that normal where you're from, to just fight 'til the death even though diplomacy exists?"

"Yeah, actually."

Bailey speeds up her walk, "You gotta be kidding me."

"No, I'm not. Remember I told you, we don't really..."

"Die. I heard you. So you all just take people off of the face of Tylon."

He taps her, and she stops. "Only those who are already killers. Her dad is an assassin, Bailey, and she is becoming one, too."

After a brief silence, Bailey responds, "Well, I can stop her from becoming one.  I will. I will stop her." She starts walking again.

"That last sentence makes more sense to me if it means permanently."

As they approach Delight's home, after stopping to grab some fries at a fast food place down the road, Eric's entire demeanor changes. He tones down, becoming laser focused on every single movement, all while Bailey is chomping on fries.

"I thought you were hungry?" she asks with her mouth full.

"I'm not understanding how you haven't lost your appetite," he mumbles.

"Because you and my dad are from Tylon. I'm from here." She stomps on the cement. "I'm from right here, and we *here* can rationalize our way through hard times and that means that I don't have to lose my appetite."

"You mean rationalize your way into self-destruction," Eric fires back.

"Whatever! Just wait and take notes. *We* aren't killers. *We* are *friends*, no matter what powers our fathers may have left us that we have and still have no idea about. All we have to do is talk about it, so I'm gonna tell her everything because honestly, Eric, that's probably why she was hesitating to come knock on my door. She probably wants to tell me the same exact thing." With that, Bailey lifts her fist, flashes a sarcastic smile at Eric and proceeds to knock the beat to her favorite song on the Delight's front door. On the second round of knocks, Delight opens the door with a bowl of ice cream in her hand.

"Hey, Bailey...and Eric. What's up?"

"Hey, Delight. Is it alright if I...we...come in?"

"Well, not really," she answers, rolling her eyes at Eric, "but I can come out. Wait. Lemme put on some sneakers." She backs away from the door and shuts it in Bailey's face.

"Just shut me out then," she responds under her breath.

"Bailey, I already told you..." Eric starts but stops when interrupted.

"I'm back!" Delight says opening the door and jumping out. "What's going on?"

"We need to talk."

"With him?"

"No...uh... Eric, can you uh..."

"Yeah, I can uh. I'll just go over here away from you two. Is that a good enough uh?" Eric answers, trying to sound as normal as possible, but in reality, he's watching Delight and plans on listening as best he can as he plants himself a short distance away, studying her every move.

"Delight, I saw you today," she lies, trying to keep Eric out of the situation. "Weren't you outside my window?"

"No. I was walking down the road, across the street from your house, but I wasn't in front of your window."

"Well, why didn't you stop?"

"I thought about it, but didn't."

Bailey rolls her eyes. "Well, why didn't you?"

Delight doesn't answer. She only stares back at Bailey like she's awaiting the next question. Therefore, Bailey assumes that Delight may need more prompting to reveal her father's secrets, assuming that was the reason she didn't cross the street like a normal best friend would have for a visit.

"Delight, listen, I know that you've probably heard from your dad, just like I've heard from mine. They've told us things that we don't like nor want to do, so because of this, we don't have to do any of it. All we have to do is be friends, just like normal."

Delight drops her head, moves the tip of her right shoe against the ground, and then speaks, "My dad has been dead for a while now, Bailey." Then, she glances up at Bailey who stands there with glimmers of hope that Delight knows and understands everything. "He's been dead long before yours...and he's still dead." Delight's face is calm and expressionless, and Bailey is in disbelief.

"Delight, cut the crap. I know. I know about us. Tylon... the whole, you know, *thing*."

"What *thing*?"

"So you're telling me right now that you don't know what I'm talking about?"

"How can I know what you're talking about when you haven't told me anything and started mentioning my dad whom you've never even met. You don't know anything about him except for what I've already told and shown you. What's this about?"

"Delight..." Bailey starts, growing more frustrated by the second, "I know you saw what I saw in the hallw..."

"Bailey, I know you're upset, but I think you might need some counseling because..."

"Bye, Delight. You're playing stupid with a situation that's not funny," she says, storming off toward Eric, before she unexpectedly feels a tap on her shoulder. She spins around angrily scowling, "What, Delight?" When she turns around, however, Delight isn't anywhere near her shoulder. In fact, she's still at the porch.

"See you in school tomorrow," Delight calls, "And I'll call you." Then she goes back inside the house and shuts the front door as Bailey stands there shaken.

"I know I felt her touch me," she whispers to herself. Suddenly, Eric appears directly behind her.

"I told you this was a bad idea. And for the record, she's practicing...like you should be doing. She did touch you. I told you, she's fast. Really fast. Let's go."

## Black Fang | Chapter Seventeen

"My mom is about to be home, Eric, so you've gotta get outta here."

"I'm not leaving until you stop me, now hurry up. You've been missing since we got here," he demands as he continues moving around the house like a character in a video game.

Already impatient and frustrated, Bailey can feel herself getting angrier watching his short locs chase him in the breeze as he races back and forth. She finally shouts, "Eric, stop!"

He looks down at his arm, and her hand is holding onto it tightly. "Well it's about time," he sings with a smile on his face. "Now you know how to do it."

"No I don't," she responds, dropping his arm and falling onto the couch, arms folded with an attitude. Her skin pulsates, and her brown skin appears to have a slightly noticeable shimmer to it. Even though she's never seen that light luster on her skin before, she completely ignores it, choosing anger and frustration over celebration and calm.

"You concentrate better when you're angry, so if you stopped me when I'm nowhere near as fast as her, then you need to make certain you're enraged when the time comes."

"The time you keep talking about is not gonna come! I can fix this."

"Wake up, Bailey!" Eric shouts, discontented with Bailey's hopeful attitude before calming back down and walking toward the front door to leave. "Just wake up." He leaves Bailey sitting straight up on the couch at attention, wondering if he's actually right. Maybe he's right. Maybe her father is correct. Maybe. Bailey's phone rings.

"Hello?"

"What was that about, Bailey?"

"Delight? Why did you call me on the home phone?"

"I just wanted to make sure you were at home, and a cell phone wouldn't do that so...and you were hanging out with Eric."

"And? Eric isn't a danger."

"And how do you know?"

"I just do. Aren't you the real danger?"

"Did he tell you that?"

"Answer the question?"

"What have I ever done to hurt you? I'm your best friend, but you know what? I'm starting to think you don't want to be that anymore."

Bailey bursts out laughing. "What on earth do you think I came to your house for today?" she asks, jumping around in a frenzy in disbelief. "I came to get rid of the obvious tension..."

"Bailey, the only tension is you. You're being weird toward me, hanging out with Eric all the time. Yeah, I was there at your house but when I saw him there..."

"Wait...you saw him?"

"Yeah."

"How did you see him?"

"Same way you did," she responds ominously, sending a chill down Bailey's spine. "My line of vision was through your curtain though," she states, breaking the eerie silence. "I guess I'm getting a little jealous that it seems you are confiding in him after your father's death and not me. I thought we were like sisters, and that's the true reason I didn't cross the street. I just decided to keep going when I saw you two."

Bailey doesn't say anything back because she doesn't know what to say. "Hold on, Delight. I need to use the bathroom." She shoves the phone underneath the red, plush pillow on the couch that used to be her dad's favorite and rushes out to Eric who's already walking down the road.

"Eric! Eric!" she shouts, waving him back. "Come back real quick."

"I thought your mom was on the way home."

"It's not about my mom," she says catching up to him. "It's about Delight. She's on the phone with me right now, and I don't know what to say."

"Say hi," he answers, annoyed that Bailey hasn't fully accepted the truth about Delight.

"Come on! Please, just come back!"

They both rush back to the house, and Bailey yanks the phone from underneath the pillow as she meets Eric outside on the porch. "Yeah, Delight, I'm back. Hello? Delight?" There's no one on the other end. "I can't believe this. She hung up the phone. I told her I would be right back and was going to use the bathroom."

"Did you not hear how loud you were calling me?"

"Yeah, to get your attention."

"I told you to wake up, Bailey. You not only got my attention, but you probably got her attention, too. Her senses are up," he continues despite feeling unheard. He, then, takes her hand gently. "I'm sorry for yelling earlier, but you really gotta take this more seriously. It could mean your life, and I don't want anything to happen to you, Bailey. I like you. You know that already."

"I'll think about everything," she shies away before going in the house.

"Do me a favor?" he asks. "Stay home tonight, and stay off the phone with Delight. That's not your friend anymore, no matter how much you want to save her."

Bailey doesn't say yes or no, but she hears him, and he can sense that she takes him seriously for the first time. Then, he looks around, and perceives who may be Bailey's mom pulling around the corner, so he returns to the original spot she called him from and continues walking as if he never left.

Instead of going back into the house, Bailey jumps from the porch and as her mom pulls in, she stops in her tracks, noticing Mrs. Conyers standing inside her house with the curtains pulled all the way back staring directly at Eric. Then, abruptly, she shuts the curtains, and Bailey drops her face into the palm of her hand, realizing that Mrs. Conyers saw Eric reach the end of the road in less than a second. Finally, she gathers her thoughts and greets her mom as usual.

"So you meet me outside today, huh?" her mother sighs, completely exhausted from work. "I had to work through lunch today, so I'm glad we have some leftovers I tucked at the bottom of the fridge."

"Yeah, Ma, I decided to meet you outside, but I'll go run your shower and fix your plate so you can lie down," she offers, wondering how she missed the other leftovers when she got home starving, though she's thankful for the salad.

"Thanks, baby. Have you been okay today?" she asks, giving her a kiss on her forehead as she walks inside the house.

"I've been better. Miss dad. I miss dad."

"I do, too, but we'll make it. We won't be moving anytime soon, but we'll make it. Don't think me and your daddy didn't know how you were knocking that sign over every day," she giggles. "Your dad thought it was funny, so when he saw you weren't in a hurry to leave, he would put the sign up for fun knowing you would knock it over. We had the house up for sale privately online anyway."

"Ma, stop playin'! You did?"

She laughs, "Yeah. I took it down. For now, this is our permanent residence until life brings us something new."

"Maybe not a new one because this one will always be my house, but we can definitely stand for life to bring us something better, better than the last couple of weeks."

"God's will, baby. His will," she responds as Bailey goes back to the shower, turns it on and then heads back into the kitchen to prepare her mom something to eat so that she can lie back in the bed and relax. Although her mom is putting on a great show for everyone else, Bailey can see the sadness and stress in her eyes, having to bear the burdens of owning a home and raising a child all alone when she used to have a strong partner, a partner stronger than what she'll ever know.

Within a couple of hours of being home, Bailey's mom falls fast asleep in her room with the television blaring and her food on the side of the bed. Therefore, Bailey turns off the TV, takes her plate into the kitchen and cleans everything up. Her mom has been going nonstop, remaining busy in order to keep from crying but as she sleeps, the tracks of tears are obviously visible on her face. As she slides the broom and dustpan behind the pantry door, she becomes startled when a sensation of another presence looms behind her. She spins around and there it is, except she doesn't know who it is, causing her to become so disturbed that she falls back onto the pantry shelves. Then, within seconds, the figure disappears.

Her heart races a mile a minute, eyes bulging from her head, as she's trapped between a state of shock and trying not to disturb her mother. Bailey grabs the broom and holds it across her chest like it's a shield, and after about ten seconds pass, she looks down at the pathetic broom in her hands.

"What?" Then, she places it back. "Wait, am I not the one with the powers in this house?" she asks herself confidently, puffing her chest out ready for anything.

"It's not enough," something whispers in her ear, and she jumps from the pantry, turning around wind-milling her arms like little children do when they fight.

"Who's there?" she asks, finally stopping her windmill and searching the air for an unseen yet heard force. Then, she stands tall attempting to magically perform some super trick that's supposed to happen when she's in danger. However, it doesn't happen. "Should I get angry?"

"Get as angry as you want," the voice whispers again, and then she recognizes it as her father.

"Dad?" she stresses under her breath.

He shoves her to the floor, and before she slams into the cabinet, her reflexes protect her, shoving her forward and off the floor like martial artists on Kung-Fu movies.

"Dad," she starts before she's shoved back down, but this time she doesn't hit the floor. She, instead, shoves herself back up with her index finger. "Stop it. If this is you, dad, quit. Mom is sleeping, and she…"

Just as she's speaking one dish goes flying across the kitchen. She quickly grabs it and puts it back. Then another goes flying, and with each dish, they fly faster and faster, forcing Bailey to move with more precision and speed…until one falls to the ground and breaks. Finally, all the movement stops.

"Dad!" she stresses for him to stop.

"Bailey!" her mom shouts, concerned after being awakened by the broken plate.

"Sorry, Ma! It's nothing!" Then, she spins around searching for her invisible dad. "Oh now you wanna stop messing with me, *after* I break a plate," she whispers. "Why didn't you decide to throw these plastic cups around?" she complains, swinging one in the air.

"Because it doesn't cost as much," he answers abruptly, startling Bailey again. "You only get one shot, and I don't want you to miss. Delight is lying to you. She knows everything, and at the right time, she will strike."

"Dad, why can't I see you? Dad? Dad?"

"Bailey?" her mom asks, standing in the dining area puzzled. Bailey stumbles back onto the counter at the sight of her mother rubbing her eyes. "Were you just calling your father?"

"Ma'am?"

Her mother walks forward to see the busted glass scattered on the kitchen floor. "How did this happen, Bailey?" she asks, leaning over to start picking up the pieces.

"No, Mom. Go back to bed. I uh... I thought I heard dad is all," she admits, leaning down to help her mother who starts giggling.

"You know what? Sometimes, I think I hear him, too. I mean, sometimes, I think he's lying next to me, and just the other night, I could have sworn his arm was around me. Crazy, huh? When you miss someone, baby, it's like that. I understand."

"Yeah." Bailey stands to toss the broken glass into the trashcan. "I figured sometimes it would be like he's still here. Sorry that I woke you up."

"Well, I'm going back to bed, and if you happen to sense your dad, tell him I love him... and that I miss him. Goodnight, baby. Sweep the floor good."

"Yes ma'am. Goodnight." When she hears her mother's room door shut, she grabs the broom and begins fussing at her father. "Dad, what is wrong with you? Aren't you supposed to be somewhere in Tylon Part Two or something?"

"I can't let you see me anymore right now. Just know I'm here. I like Eric by the way."

Shocked, her eyes bolt open and her mouth drops. "Dad, you were watching us? Really? Will you stop? That is disgusting...not that we were doing anything... but can I have some privacy?"she asks, sweeping the glass across the floor. "Ouch!" She steps on a small piece of glass and pulls it from her foot. "Daddy!" she calls in a whisper. "See what you made me do!" When she looks back at her wound, it's all healed up, like she'd never been cut.

"You needed to know. Bye, Bailey baby."

Immediately, she glances up with tears welling up inside her eyes and her body releasing an immense sadness before she utters, "Thank you, Daddy. I love you. Bye."

After getting herself and the floor together, she goes back into her bedroom and calls Eric. The phone rings until the voicemail answers, so she ends the call and dials again. This time, he picks up.

"Yeah, Bailey. What's up?"

"I heal! I heal like super fast in like less than a second!"

"Good."

"And it was my dad that showed me that I heal. He made me drop a dish and when I cut myself, I healed!"

"You saw him again?"

"No, but he spoke to me...and he saw you."

"What?!" Eric shouts. "What do you mean? Your dad saw me? Like with you?"

"Right! I'm so embarrassed."

"Wait a minute. Why...uh...why are you embarrassed?"

"What?" Bailey asks confused.

"I mean, I...uhh..."

"Noo!" she sighs, dropping her head into her pillow. "I mean, I'm just embarrassed that he saw us and was listening to us, you know, watching. I'm not embarrassed about you. Why on earth would you think that I was..."

"My bad, you know, I'm just thinking..."

"Don't think. Anyway, did you not hear what I just said?"

"About your healing? Yeah, that's good. I don't think it'll heal that fast from super deep wounds though. Flesh wounds, scrapes and scars, small punctures and that sort of thing, not through the body type damage."

"Oh, I was kind of hoping."

"Don't hope. No one survives that, but don't think about *not* surviving anything. The number one rule of Tylon is either conquer or win. That's also a problem because everyone believes it and strives for it, even the worst of us, meaning it makes our battles brutal at times because surrender isn't an option. It's almost criminal."

"I'm really going to have to fight her, aren't I?" she asks, slumping down into the mattress.

"Yeah, you will, and about your body healing fast. You heal as a direct response to not wasting your blood. Your blood is powerful, especially to our ill-fated, evil cousins. If Delight touches it, you not only feel it, but it empowers them, almost like a vampire thirsts for blood on movies. I'm not certain how it works, but it does. Lonthians' genetic makeup change somehow over the course of time, and when it combines with ours, it unleashes something in them that I don't quite understand."

"Does it happen to you? Your healing?"

"Yeah, but maybe not as fast as yours. It depends. Maybe I heal in two to ten minutes or so. I haven't had to heal in a while."

"That's fast, Eric," Bailey says rolling her eyes.

"Nah. You healed in... what did you say... seconds? That's fast. I'm a sluggish healer in comparison. That means I have an even greater chance at death, so you don't have to worry about me fighting you," he jokes. "I love my life out here."

"Is it really that hard to fight us?"

"Bailey...yes. Hard is an understatement."

# Black Fang | Chapter Eighteen

For several days after school, Bailey and Eric meet at a nearby park to practice for what he continues to call the Day of War. Bailey believes it's corny, but Eric continues to tell her that it's supposed to sound corny because he isn't trying to make it sound cool.

"I'm trying to save your life, Bailey," he says as they both take a break on the grass next to the pond. "And you better believe if I can help it, I won't let anything happen to you. You have my word."

"I have your word?" Bailey responds, smiling while hoping her dad isn't listening in from behind some pockets of air. "Even after all this practicing we've been doing, you still think I'm a softy?"

"Nah. I think you're hardcore. I think you mean what you say, and I know you put your heart into everything you do and everyone you care about. I love people like that."

Bailey blushes and looks away. "You love *people* like that?"

"Honestly, I love that about you."

Standing from the grass, she inhales, trying not to connect more with him than she already has, and right as she's about to respond to what she knows is a romantic advance, she feels his presence standing directly behind her. At that, she turns around to face him and nearly melts because she's grown even more attracted to him, his dark brown eyes, his height, his short black locs, all the way down to how he treats and protects her.

As he stands there before her in adoration of her picture perfect face, irresistible brown eyes and curly hair, he asks, "What is it about me that you love?"

"Everything," she answers, but as soon as the word comes out, she hears something behind a tree near the water's edge and turns to look. Eric turns to look as well.

"I heard that, too." He then closes his eyes for a few seconds, and then reopens them. "It's fine."

"What did you do?" she asks, noticing how he shut his eyes momentarily.

"I can see, sort of like in reverse, whenever I close my eyes... like I can swing the land around to see behind it. I can't see through things, but I can see around them."

"So you look around it?"

"Sort of. So see," he explains. "I'm standing here and facing in this same direction. If I shut my eyes, the land in front of me turns like a door opening and shutting, and I can see the other side. It's the best way I can explain it. I can't see through things, but…"

"But you can flip it to the other side."

"Exactly. My mind sort of takes a picture of the whole area and turns it around like a 3D visual on a computer or something like that."

"Wow. Can I try? Is there a special thing you do?"

He smiles. "No, I just close my eyes. I think it has to do with my focus."

Bailey concentrates, shuts her eyes for about five seconds and opens them. "Well, that's not my gift."

"You don't need it. I'll hold on to it for you. Let's go," he says, taking her by the hand as they leave the area, however, as they leave, Eric glances back, shutting his eyes once more, realizing that they aren't alone, despite the fact that he still sees no one there.

"You alright?" she asks, noticing how he looked back.

"Yeah, I'm good."

"So, how do you think I'm doing? I mean, I didn't catch you every time, but …"

"I think you are much better when angry. When you got frustrated, just like the other day when we were in your house, you did much better. If you get angry, you will dominate. Thing is, you need to think about the worst thing, anything that makes you furious, not just upset. If you can do this, you won't have to worry too much about Delight."

"When do you think she will try and attack me?"

"I don't know. Just keep your eyes open and remember to make yourself angry when it happens. You have to let that friend stuff go somehow. That's what makes her so dangerous to you, Bailey. You care too much. Tell you the truth though, I think she was here."

"Seriously?"

"Yeah. I think so. That's why I'm whispering."

Bailey stops, turns around and calls her. "Delight? Delight!" She waits, but she gains no response as she searches between the trees. She then turns back around, looks at Eric, shrugs and continues walking along side him. As they walk away, Delight stands in the background, internally fighting against what she knows to be her friend versus her father and the memory of his death that she has seen repeatedly in her mind and the vengeance she is compelled to take.

She's been struggling with herself all alone for days, and sometimes, even when looking in the mirror, she doesn't fully recognize herself. The power and the rage come up all at once, and the only time there is somewhat peace is when she's asleep. However, in the middle of the night, she wakes up crying and out of breath, like the life is being choked from her, and she has no idea why.

As she stands there beneath the trees longing for the way things used to be with Bailey, she's overpowered by the force of her father. Delight's longing to call her and tell her the truth about everything is overpowered by the betrayal she feels each time she watches, and even feels, death barreling down on the man who brought her life. Tears flow from her eyes as she blocks out her anguish by rapidly searching for any traces of Bailey's blood that may have somehow spilled in order to give her even more strength in the fight that is yet to come.

"Mom?" Delight calls when she enters her house, finally returning from the park. Everything is quiet, but when she calls her mother again, she answers.

"I'm back here, sweetheart. I'm trying to adjust this gown I'm making for a bride that's getting married in a couple of days. She doesn't want the front of the dress dragging the floor. She went and changed shoes, and the heels are shorter than the previous pair," she continues as Delight pops into the doorway of a bedroom that her mother made into her office. Her mother is a seamstress as a side job with hopes of making it her full-time business soon. "What's going on?"

"I think I'm changing."

Her mother smiles. "How so? You do remember that first big change you already went through. Do you think you're going through another one so fast, baby?" she laughs. "Menopause should be decades away."

"Not that. I think it's...I feel like dad is closer to me, more than when he was even in life."

Her mother stops the gown alteration and sits back in the chair in silence before telling her daughter to explain. Delight walks over slowly, extremely nervous about telling her mother everything, so she carefully delivers her thoughts as she sits on the chair directly across from her mom on the other side of the room. Her posture is perfect, from her toes to her pointed chin. Her shoulders are back and her fingers lay in perfect alignment on her lap while she watches her perfectionist mother's approval.

"Ma, I just feel really different. I'm angry at people I shouldn't have any anger for most of the time, and whenever I think about it, I get really sad because I don't have a reason to be mad at them because they didn't do anything to me... and then there's dad."

"Who is they, and what does that have to do with your father?"

"The *they* I'm angry with are some classmates, and I don't know exactly how it has to do with dad," she fabricates. "I just feel like he's somehow near whenever I get angry, and mom, I get really angry. It feels like I need to take something out on..."

"It sounds like you're mourning, Delight. Your father passed away not that long ago and now Bailey's. Maybe that triggered something inside you," she interrupts, drifting off. "But what about Bailey? Since her father's funeral, I haven't heard you two talking as much or seen you texting each other as much. Before, all you would ever talk about is Bailey. Now, who are these other people who have become so extremely important to you that you are angry at them, that you even care what they think or say?"

"I don't care about what people think about me, Ma," Delight moans, irritated because she can't get her mother to understand.

"Good."

"I'm just angry. I'm just angry all the time. Even when I try and shake it, it's still there."

"Don't be. It's just a feeling, an emotion. Don't blame the emotion on your father either," she orders, staring her directly into her eyes. "Be angry instead at the circumstance that took him away from you, that is if you're going to be angry. Evil is ugly, Delight. He was murdered. Be angry at murder. Be angry at evil. You're angry because he's gone, and honestly, I'm sure he's angry that he's gone, too. Now is the time for self-control. Self-control is as close as you or I can get to maintaining all control, even in your father's death. Do you understand me?"

"Yes, Ma, I do. It's hard."

"Your hormones may be going a bit out of sorts, too, but they will organize. But let me ask you again," she continues, leaning forward as if she's studying Delight, in search of hidden truths that she knows are there. "Because I didn't get an answer, so let me rephrase it. When did you and Bailey stop hanging out?"

"What?"

"You heard me, Delight," she responds with a slight smile as she glances at the hardwood floor.

"We do hang out."

"You know what I mean," she says, turning back to hem the gown. "I know you may not want to tell me everything, but whenever you fall out with your best friend in the entire world, you may feel angry, Delight. I've noticed the distance between you two. You're normally texting away all night, but now, your phone has no incoming or outgoing. I don't have to spy on you to notice that."

Delight doesn't know what to say because her mother is right. Everything between her and Bailey is changing, and it's changing at a rapid pace. As she sits silently, she can tell that her mother senses her apprehension. "Ma, sometimes I feel like doing bad things, really bad things."

Her mom doesn't bat an eye. She continues focusing on the task in between her fingertips, and when she finally lifts her head to respond, Delight is already gone, regretting she even said a word. With her mother, it's either strength or nothing, but Delight doesn't want to be this type of strong. It's the wrong type, and soon she fears she won't be able to fight it because with each sight of Bailey, her feelings worsen. It's becoming harder to fake a smile, walk next to her or even be in the same classroom without an insatiable urge to attack.

# Black Fang | Chapter Nineteen

"Okay, class! I need to you hear me and remember, not just hear me and let it go into one ear and out the other. This assignment needs to be completed by Monday, no exceptions. This bell may be ringing, but you need to hear me and have it completed."

"But, Mrs. Perkins, you just assigned it to us today," a student complains as he stands up from his desk, gathering his things as the bell continues to sound.

"And you will have it done by Monday. It's Thursday. Maybe you think the due date should be tomorrow, Raymond?"

"Monday, Mrs. Perkins, Monday," he replies as the other students in the class shout at him to be quiet before he makes it worse.

"You all have cellular phones. If you can't meet up in person, I suggest you call your partners on video and collaborate like that. Just get it done. Instead of endlessly scrolling on social media, use those phones for work. See you tomorrow!"

Bailey and Delight exit the class together, despite the fact that they didn't select each other for the project. Everyone else selected their partners, and they assumed the best friends would choose each other. Therefore, they didn't bother searching for a teammate. Their union was is automatic.

"So looks like we're stuck together," Bailey says to break the ice, "And I'm assuming we're gonna decide on this twentieth century topic today?"

"Yeah, I was already thinking something like something out of the Harlem Renaissance, some of the female artists maybe? And why do you say that?"

"Say what?"

"Stuck together," she replies before they part ways for their next classes. "You say it like we haven't always been together. You're like my sister. As a matter of fact, you are my sister. We're like...blood."

"Yeah, like blood," Bailey pauses, getting a flashback of how she felt Delight touch her blood while standing at her front door. "We are like sisters, and..."

"And it's all good. Unfortunately, all this happened because your father passed away. That's the only reason why things are awkward and icky. Don't you agree?"

"Yes. I agree. I..."

"Your house or mine?" Delight purposely interrupts.

"Maybe the public library or something, or we can do what Mrs. Perkins said back there...call each other social media or..."

"Library closes too early. How about Saturday evening ... at my house?"

"Is your mom gonna be there?"

"I don't know. Does she need to be? It's our project. We have goals to meet, right?"

"Right," Eric states as he walks up behind Bailey. "Goals. Me and Bailey, we have relationship goals! Isn't that what you ladies call it?" he jokes purposely, having been listening to the whole conversation from down the hall.

Delight smiles at him, and as she smiles, her eyes remain on him while telling Bailey what time to meet her. "Between four and six maybe. I'll call you. I guess now I'll let you and your boyfriend go."

"Who said he's my..."

"Come on, Bailey." Eric grabs her hand and escorts her from the conversation because Delight has already left it.

"She's just upset that we are spending so much time together, and she's left out."

"It's good to know you still care about covering for her, but she's all in."

"All in what?"

"Your destruction ... and you speak too soon. You have to wait until she's out of radius. You still can't use your hypersonic ears yet?"

"I have them?"

"Yeah, all of us do to a certain degree."

"Well, that must be the last thing to develop on me."

"Maybe. Listen, before Saturday night, you need to imagine every possible scenario because your accepting this project date is an acceptance to fight for your life."

"Eric, it's in her house. There's not gonna be any fight in her house. Chill. Could you imagine?"

"No, I couldn't, but what if it's made to look like an accident?"

Bailey stops. "I didn't think about that."

"See. You need me."

"Maybe I should fill my stomach before I go, in case she tries to poison me."

"And take your own drink."

"Exactly."

"Whatever you do, just be careful. I have to run to class, but don't get caught up in speaking to her like normal. Keep it business, school business. If possible, don't even go on Saturday."

"Bye, Eric."

"Later."

Throughout her classes, Bailey can't concentrate. All of her thoughts are on Delight, and how this may be the end, the real end. To Bailey, everything feels like her actions are being orchestrated in a story book and she's some character. No matter how much she tries to avoid the confrontation between her and her best friend, it seems like it's still inevitable, like she has no control over any outcome.

Sadness creeps over her body. Every second that goes by vibrates through her body like a heartbeat, and she finds herself paying more attention to it than classroom instruction. Her pen hasn't moved the entire time, and there are formulas all over the white board. She sees them, but none of it makes any sense. Then, something goes wrong.

"Bailey? Oh my goodness, Bailey! Someone help me get her up. Bailey!" the teacher runs toward the back of the room as Bailey is being lifted from the floor by a couple of students. "Bailey, what happened? Are you okay?" the teacher asks. "You have to go to the nurse. Will you walk her to the nurse, please? Let me go write you an excuse," the teacher says, walking off as Bailey's head defogs.

"I don't know what just happened," Bailey manages to reply as she stands from the floor while everyone is grabbing at her arms to steady her. "I think I'm fine, guys. I don't know what happened. I mean, I just think I passed out."

"Here," the teacher says handing her a hall pass. "Go to the nurse's office and get checked out. You two, walk her, and come straight back," she orders two students as she proceeds teaching again. One of the students lifts her book bag and the other walks close to Bailey, making certain that she is steady on her feet. By the time, Bailey reaches the nurse's office, she feels perfectly fine, but must still be examined.

"I see you passed out," she states, reading the note from Bailey's teacher. "Go ahead and sit up here on the table so I can check your reflexes. Have you been feeling okay lately?" she asks as she retrieves a mallet.

"I've been feeling fine, a little stressed but fine."

"Is it school work giving you that little bit of stress?"

"Yes, school work," Bailey lies.

"Will you open your mouth for me wide and say ah?"

Bailey does, and the nurse checks the back of her throat, asks her to breathe while she checks her heart with a stethoscope and then checks her temperature. Finally, the nurse pulls up a stool and sits.

"Everything is checking out, but the question is really something that I can't test. How do you feel? Do you still feel like you can go throughout the school day, or should you call a family member to pick you up? I would hate for you to take a fall in these hallways if you are unsteady on your feet."

"I walked here fine. I don't know what really happened. I was seated in my desk, and then, I just went over."

"Let me check your blood sugar."

"With a needle?" Bailey panics because she hates needles.

"No. Technology. Hold still. Did you eat breakfast?"

"No."

"How about dinner last night?"

"A little bit."

"Well, it looks like a sugar boost may get you more stable though your blood sugar is okay. Here. Drink this orange juice and eat a sandwich, one of the subs for lunch, which is in about thirty minutes. If you feel the same, come back to me. Here's a pass in case you need to use it."

Bailey slides from the table, and even though she takes the hall pass, she decides to go home. She has no vision beyond Delight, and because of that, she has no reason to remain in classes. Her mind is completely blanketed by what ifs and the inevitable confrontation that both her father and Eric insist will happen.

As she leaves the nurse's office, Eric appears in the hallway, and she rolls her eyes jokingly. "You're skipping class again."

"Nah. You are my class for now. I got sick, too, so I could find you."

"How did you know I was here?"

"Texts travel fast about a girl that passed out in class named Bailey."

"Now, I know I'm not going back to class. I'm gonna call my mom actually, so I don't need you to walk me or get yourself an absence because of me."

"Well, let me walk you to the office, and I'll finish up with class right after since you care so much about my education," he clowns with a huge smile.

"Shut up," Bailey laughs, but it fades into a whisper. "I'm scared, Eric." Tears well up in her eyes, and they find their way down her cheeks in front of him. She immediately wipes them away. "I'm not a fighter nor am I a..."

"You're right. You're not, Bailey, so don't. You don't have to do it, alright? You don't."

"How? Why do you say that now when since my dad died, that's all the goal is – Bailey will fight?!"

"I got you. Don't worry about it."

"What do you mean?"

"I said, don't worry about it. I won't let anything happen to you, alright? And trust me, you won't make the choice. I've made it for you, okay, so you have to trust me."

"Trust you?"

"Yeah, trust me because you're not ready. Tell me that you trust me."

"I trust ... I will trust you ... soon ... I hope."

"Good enough. Try and get in touch with your father, too. I know he's listening anyway."

"You think?"

"If I was a father, I would."

"Now that you say that..." she stalls, but adds, "But, Eric, there's something else."

"What?"

"About this weekend..."

"What is it?"

"It's Delight's eighteenth birthday."

"You gotta be kidding," he groans.

"No. Thing is, she isn't even talking about it. We haven't planned anything. It's like it's not even on her mind. To be honest, it hasn't been on my mind either. Do you really think...no, you know what? She's salty!"

"Salty?"

"Yeah, because she thinks I've forgotten about the whole thing."

Eric sighs. "Maybe. That's a high possibility."

"I'm gonna get her something, maybe put things on the mend? I mean, we haven't been speaking much, and any other time, I'm with you.

I've been her only real friend since she moved here, and that's most the main reason why I didn't want my parents to sell the house. She's like my sister, Eric, and honestly, you're taking up her spot. Now, she has no one."

"Everything you say makes sense, but don't get your hopes up, Bailey. Remember everything we said. None of this is a coincidence. Your father isn't a liar, and neither am I. You're grasping at straws..."

"Well let me grasp," she snaps, and Eric falls silent not wanting to upset her anymore as well because he senses her father may be watching and he wants to make a great impression.

When they arrive at the office, Eric gives her a light kiss on the forehead, and she enters the office alone though he waits outside in the hallway for a couple minutes before leaving.

"May I sign out of school, please? I'm not feeling too good, and I need to go home."

"Sure, do you have a note from the nurse, and have you already called your parents?"

"Yes, ma'am, I do, and I'm sending her a message right now to come get me."

"Wait here, and she'll have to sign you out."

"I'm gonna step outside the door and go to the restroom."

"That's fine. Just stay close by."

"Okay." As she leaves the office and enters the restroom, she whips out her phone and texts Delight:


*I can't wait to celebrate ur bday with u. Ur turning 18 finally! I'll be right around the corner from u next yr.*


From there, Bailey waits in the bathroom which she notices is quite smelly, so she creeps back over toward the bathroom's entrance so that she can inhale fresher air. Finally, while fiddling with her phone, a text message comes through and it's from Delight.

*I thought u forgot, and I wasn't gonna make a big deal out of it being that ur already dealing w more imp. things. U don't have to bring me a gift this weekend. It won't be necessary.*

Stunned at the words *it won't be necessary,* Bailey impulsively texts Eric.

*Ur right. I'm just not gonna go to her house, Eric. I'm gonna avoid her.*

Not wanting to read his response, she shoves her phone in her back pocket as it vibrates multiple times. She imagines him saying *I told you so* or *smh.* She has a sinking feeling in the pit of her stomach that confirms this, but she prefers to pass out again instead of face it.

Exiting the bathroom, she goes back into the office and sits on the smooth, leather seats until her mother enters the office after about forty minutes. She walks in, oblivious to Bailey sitting there and signs her out. When she finally does notice Bailey, she breathes a sigh of relief and rushes to her.

"Are you alright? You passed out, baby. What did the nurse say?"

"She gave me some orange juice. Stress probably, Mom. I feel better now, much better."

"Come on. Let's go. Get you home and make you some soup. Do you have some vitamins left?"

"Yeah, I have enough. I didn't take the dose this morning, and I didn't eat either so..."

"Bailey, I've told you about skipping meals. You're gonna have these people believing..."

"No. I'm not two years old. No one will believe you aren't feeding me. I skipped. That's all."

"Don't skip," her mother responds sternly. "That's an order. I've already lost your father, and I can't bear something happening to you."

Those words echo in Bailey's ears as she gets into the car, and all the way home, her heart aches because she can't allow anything to happen to herself to spare her mother, and she can't fight Delight. She just can't, no matter how much she may need to do so.

## Black Fang | Chapter Twenty

On Friday, all Bailey did was argue back and forth with Eric via text message. It was their first real argument because despite Bailey saying that she wasn't going to Delight's house, she changed her mind after deciding to hang out with her both in and afterschool that day. Bailey and Delight were getting along so great that she even let Delight in on the fact that she and Eric were arguing, but she didn't let her know exactly what it was about. Now that it's Saturday afternoon, the argument continues but less severe.

"I like your other idea. At least it gives you more time," he explains, hoping to convince her to give up meeting with Delight.

"Time for what? You know something? My body hasn't been flinching or doing anything like before. My teeth, even though I have an extra set of fangs, feel fine. Even Delight, she is acting back to normal. Maybe the timeframe we were supposed to feel like this is over. Is there a time frame?"

"Honestly, I don't know everything about this, but your father would not have lied. Just don't go to her house like you said, but if you decide to go, lemme come with you."

"Eric, no," she sighs. "I already got her a present, and I'm walking there on my own. It's a nice day, and I need to think. At the most, I'll text you when I get there."

"When are you leaving?"

"Now actually. It's four o'clock, and my mom is picking me up later. It's all good."

"Bye, Bailey, and be careful."

"Of course. Aren't you the one that told me my hormones will kick in and protect me automatically?"

"Yeah, only if you see it coming. Remember that." There's a silence... a this-is-the-end silence which prompts Eric to say one more thing. "I feel like I need to say something."

"Yeah, I do, too."

"I uhh...care about you," he announces, stressing the word care.

"I care about you, too, Eric. Bye." She ends the call, smiles slightly at the thought of their conversation, inhales, exhales, grabs her bag and Delight's present and leaves, deciding to skip the long route and take a short cut. The short cut is through a cobblestone, arched walkway, and since it's still daylight, Bailey decides to take that route.

By the time she arrives at the walk-through, she passes by a couple exiting. Therefore, she slides to the other side of the walkway to allow a couple to pass. At the sight of them, she fantasizes about Eric and being coupled with him. It brings another huge gush of happiness across her heart as she arrives to the end of the pathway. Across two streets and two blocks down is Delight's house, and when she finally arrives, she gathers the gift in her hand, and rings the doorbell, ready to scream happy birthday and get at least some of their project done.

Rocking back and forth in front of the door, she's optimistic about everything. No matter what has been going on, she feels that she's in no danger while waiting outside what is supposed to be home of her arch nemesis. She even giggles because she's not getting any intense feelings like she believes she would get if there is actually danger lurking behind the door.

She rings the doorbell again, looking around, even starting to wonder if the doorbell is actually working. Therefore, she rings it again before using her cell phone to make a call.

"Come on, Delight..." she says, excited to try and regain some sense of normalcy after having such a great day with her yesterday in school, however, Delight never picks up the phone. Finally, she backs away from the door, and sits on the step, making excuses for why she may not be answering the door. "Toilet, on the way back home from somewhere, sleep," she continues to rattle off before finally getting back up to knock on the door. To her surprise again, no one is coming to answer the door at all, therefore, she decides to call Eric.

"Hello, Eric?"

"Yeah, what's up?"

"Can you believe I'm out here at Delight's house to meet her for the assignment and her birthday, and she isn't even at home. I put my ear up to the door and everything."

"Leave," he says calmly.

"But..."

"Just leave. Go back home. Did you send her a text?"

"I am right now as I'm talking to you, but I did call her. Still, I got nothing."

"I wouldn't wait there too long. Fact is, she isn't there, and you don't need to be there. You never know what's going on, and it's getting later by the second. Head on back home."

"You're right. This makes no sense. I'll call you when I get back."

"Bet."

They end the call, and Bailey lets out a huge groan of frustration, looks at the gift that's inside her hand and then heads back home in disbelief that not only is Delight not home but they also have a big project to present in class next week that won't get done. On the way back, the streets aren't as crowded as they once were, possibly because the bus had already made its stop. Therefore, in a split decision,

Bailey decides to take that same short cut back home to walk off her irritation instead of waiting on the next bus. However, as soon as she gets to the alleyway, although it's clear with no people in sight, she feels someone is watching her, almost breathing down her neck. Quickly, she turns around, but no one is there. From there, she shoves Delight's gift in her pocket and starts down the alleyway.

Suddenly, her mouth starts to throb, and she stops in pain. When she reaches up to touch her gums, there's blood. "Oh no," she whispers and then feels a touch on her arm, but no one is there. "What's going on?" When she turns back around, she runs into something, or to be more accurate, something unseen runs into her, causing her to fall to the gravel. It finally hits her. It's Delight.

# Black Fang | Chapter Twenty-One

"Sorry, Bailey," Delight sings with a huge, mischievous grin on her face finally revealing herself. "I think I may have missed you when you stopped by. Are you ready to do the class work?" she continues, slowly walking around Bailey as if she's a hound on two legs sniffing.

Immediately, Bailey is keenly aware that she isn't at all safe, so believing that she can tone the tension down, she reveals the gift she bought her. "Happy birthday, Delight. I got you this..." but as she speaks, a tiny drop of blood mysteriously drips from her tooth onto her lip.

"Oh what's that?" Delight curiously asks, leaning over to inspect closer, and when she sees it's blood, she rapidly reaches up to touch it. Bailey moves back but is far too slow.

"It's my tooth. It's irritated."

"Irritated?" Delight asks as she caresses the blood in between her fingertips. "Don't be!" She swiftly moves behind Bailey, so quick that Bailey doesn't see her, but only hears the giggling from behind. "Did you ever imagine?" she asks, "Your blood..." she continues, lifting her bloody finger in close proximity to her mouth and then blowing onto it. As soon as the respiration hits the blood, Bailey feels a chill. "It's like an extension of you," she explains, shrugging happily as fear grips Bailey who is realizing slowly that this particular Delight isn't the one from yesterday. It's the Delight that her father and Eric told her about though ... the Delight that she will have to fight.

Bailey takes a deep breath, and Delight doesn't miss it. She traces every particle in the air and notices that they don't separate and she laughs before saying, "Watch this!" She then, slams the tip of her bloody index finger against the brick wall of the alleyway, and it immediately feels like a hammer hits Bailey directly in her side, causing her to fall onto the ground, wheezing for air as Delight becomes tickled at her struggle.

Then, she falls down next to Bailey and asks, "Are you okay? It appears that you can't breathe." At those words she sucks the oxygen from the area surrounding Bailey, and just as the dog walker did the other day, Bailey struggles to breathe and chokes in desperation.

"Do you like my new tricks? I do," she laughs. "I figured that today, my birthday, would be the day I take the ultimate revenge ... for my father ... the man that your dad took away from me, and now, I'm gonna take you away." Her face goes expressionless. "Happy birthday to me." She disappears, and just as Bailey is just catching her breath, in one blink, Delight hovers over her in preparation for a forceful knife-hand strike when Delight is suddenly slammed into the same brick wall that she used against Bailey.

"Bailey, get up. She parts the air, so take a deep breath before she inhales." It's Eric.

"Eric," Bailey pants out of breath. "I can't fight her."

"Don't let her take your breath. Now, get up!" he shouts as Delight charges him at high speed, and before Bailey's eyes, they battle a battle like she's never seen before.

"Delight, stop! Delight!" she shouts, but there's no response, and finally she notices that Eric isn't fighting her. Delight is trying to kill her, but

Eric is creating a transparent shield, or barrier, to keep her protected as Delight shatters each section he erects. Immediately, she gets up and thinks of anything that makes her angry, but the fear she has also gets in the way. Concentrating seems too much for her, but something happens that changes all that. Eric slows down to look at her, and that's when Delight strikes him across his face. The strike is so hard that Eric is thrown to the other side of the alleyway, and he doesn't get back up. Delight sets her eyes back on Bailey, and the sight she sees is a completely different foe.

"There you are!" Delight laughs. "Is that what it takes for you to actually wake up? Knocking your little boyfriend out? Guess what my dad told me? Eric can't beat me. Guess who's the only one who stands a chance? That's another reason why *you* have to go." She crouches down to the ground and prepares to place her index finger on what Bailey notices is a small drop of her blood, and she lunges directly toward what is now her foe. Delight moves and laughs hysterically.

"You know I saw your dad kill mine in your eyes that day in the hallway. You showed that to me on purpose, so that means that you've always known."

"That's a lie, Delight. I had no idea," Bailey argues back.

"Oh yes you did. My father told me everything. You've always known. You played me, like you were my sister. You're nothing to me."

"Your father is a liar."

Delight furiously attacks, and Bailey fights back, blocking every hit and creating every miss. Her blood pulsates through her entire body, throughout the tips of her fingernails to the bottoms of her feet. Her skin changes to a smoother texture in the heat of battle, and even her eyes turn blood red. She's never been this focused and enraged at the same time, and finally, she strikes Delight with a powerful blow to the chest. Delight stumbles back.

"I never knew about your dad until my dad died! He told me that your father was an assassin and that he fled Tylon. My dad followed him because he was a law keeper, and when they found each other, he had to kill him. My dad would and could never kill anyone unless he had to do it!"

"He didn't *have to do* anything! That was my father!" Delight screams in agony.

"My dad had no choice! Your dad was going to kill him!"

"Like he should have!" Delight growls as she attacks again, fully engaged, as she begins to suck in air, but Bailey remembers what Eric said and leaps from the area to inhale before fiercely blocking every attack made by Delight. Unfortunately, she glances at Eric lying there on the ground, loses focus and she's careened into the brick wall by Delight's fist.

Her head never hurt so bad, and her body never felt so broken. The pain ripping through her body is great, but within seconds, she feels it healing, and as she watches Delight come at full speed with her right hand clawed and coming for her throat, something takes over her body. In a split second, Bailey's jaw tightens to the point of excruciating pain, and in the next second, as Delight's claw is inches from her throat, a bold thrust shoves her head forward, her mouth connecting directly between Delight's neck and shoulder. At the connection, the fangs in Bailey's mouth sharply pierces four inches into Delight's body, and then retracts instantly, as her claw grabs Bailey's neck and squeezes. Within seconds, it goes weak while the poison from Bailey's fangs circulates in her body.

Delight then, in a state of desperation, pushes forward despite the bite, trying her best to crush Bailey's throat, but Bailey easily removes Delights hand from her throat, and as her best friend abhors her like a vicious animal, she suddenly rips Bailey's left fang from her mouth. A gripping pain tears through Bailey's face as she loses control once again, but seconds later, she attacks once again as her single fang digs directly into Delight's chest. Her other fang falls to the ground as blood pours from her mouth while Delight dangles inside of Bailey's grip.

"You win again." Delight smiles as life leaves her, and she dies in Bailey's arms. Distraught, Bailey goes to the ground with her closest friend, squeezing her tightly, rocking back and forth, begging for forgiveness, screaming that she didn't mean it.

"Daddy, why did you do this to me?" she hollers as Delight never returns and he never answers. She then gathers the birthday present that she bought for her. It's a heart pendant. She takes one half of the heart and places it around Delight's neck before placing the other half on hers, and with tears flowing down her face, she whispers, "Happy Birthday."

"Eric?" she calls, noticing movement from his body as she cradles Delight's body before carefully laying her on the ground. Then, she rushes to him, slightly shaking him in hopes that he responds. "Eric, come on now. I just saw you move."

"That's because I did," he groans. "You really don't know the beating I was taking, do you?" He lifts up his shirt and shows the multiple bruises as they slowly fade away. "Don't worry, I'm almost all patched up."

"Oh thank God!"

"Amen!" he smiles, then he takes a look at the fallen Delight, and reaches up to take Bailey's hand. "That wasn't her."

"I know," Bailey responds, too emotional to say anything else. Then she notices that the fang that was ripped from her mouth is missing. It's no longer on the ground. Therefore, she scrambles away in a panic searching for it as Eric regains the strength to stand on his own. As he watches her search for her fang, he sees people from his periphery. It's twins, a boy and a girl, licking huge lollipops staring directly at them. The street lights come on, and the two children look up, and take off running back home.

"Bailey," Eric stalls "we have to go."

"I can't find my fang. My fang...it was right here."

"What?" he panics, and begins searching with her.

"I saw where it landed. It was right here. It was right here, Eric!" she stresses as he pulls her along.

"We have to go. It's not there anymore. We have to go. Bailey, your mouth ... your face ... come on before anyone else sees us."

"People saw us?"

"No ... but yeah. Just walk with your head down. I got you. Keep your head down. Walk fast. Don't talk to me. Just walk. Head down..."

"I heard you! She's just laying back there, Eric! We need to call for help!" she cries feeling like her whole entire world is crumbling. She attempts to look back at Delight, but he reminds her again.

"Look down! Stay with me. If I stop, you stop."

"Why?"

"I have you covered."

"Covered?"

"Yeah. That's the whole reason why you saw no one and no one saw you or me for the most part. I had to create like three fields around us. It blinds people, but I'm not good at it. I learned the trick from an old friend in Tylon. Be quiet so I can concentrate."

Bailey wipes her eyes and walks, not understanding what's going to happen next, afraid of everything. When they reach the house, her mother isn't at home, and she flies to the bathroom, jumps in the shower and changes clothes while Eric waits outside in the front yard. Her face and mouth are healing fast, and as she shoves her clothes in the dirty clothes hamper, she falls to the floor and cries. Two minutes go by, and an amazing itch develops in the center of her chest. Although she rubs really hard, the itch won't disappear. It feels like it's coming from inside her body instead of the outside.

Finally, she remembers that Eric is outside and that her mother is coming home, so she quickly cleans off her face and dashes into the living room, then she texts her mother:

*Mom, just to let u know, I'm already at home.*

Then, she walks back outside to Eric...and the lady across the street shutting her curtains just enough to not be rude while she's staring.

"You alright?"

"No. I'm not alright, but I can't show it at all, can I?"

"Definitely not. At least you look like your normal self again."

"My normal self? "

"Yeah, your face changes whenever... you know."

"No, no, I don't," she says walking directly in front of him.

"It's more angular and..."

She drops her head in shame. "Oh my gosh. I look like a monster."

"No, no, it's not like that. It's more defined, more beautiful. And don't worry," he starts again, "You're unrecognizable whenever you are actively completing a mission. If somehow someone saw you change, which I doubt because I believe I prevented it, no one will ever come looking for you. Don't be afraid."

"She really tried to kill me."

"Yeah. You did nothing wrong. It was self-defense, Bailey. It was gonna be you or her. What's wrong?" he asks, noticing her rubbing her chest furiously.

"I'm itching bad, like something is beneath my skin."

"Oh okay, just do yourself a favor, and don't watch the news. Let someone else come tell you whenever it hits. Prepare yourself, Bailey, and remember... you're of Tylon, too."

"Thanks for saving my life, Eric, but what about my blood?"

"It's only of Tylon when you battle. Your blood and her blood changed when you two were active, but now that she isn't active, she... but they can't track you at all. I told you that I wouldn't let anything happen to you." He leans over and kisses her on her cheek and leaves.

She stands there for only a couple minutes before her mom pulls around the corner. Tapping her face and hair, she continues to hold back her agony with a fake smile as the sight of her deceased friend destroys her thoughts. She continues to tell herself that she had no choice, but did she? Every scenario plays through her mind, and finally a voice says, "Girl, if you don't stop daydreaming, and come help me get these groceries. So that was fast. How's Delight?"

"Oh...hey, Ma." she answers, moving slowly to unload the rest of the groceries from the trunk. Her mother notices through her own intuition that something is wrong. Before going inside the house, she glances back at Bailey and asks, "Are you okay, baby?"

Bailey stops in the fresh, green lawn. "It's dad, that's all."

Her mother slumps her shoulders, walks back over to Bailey, touches her face gently and reassures her that in time, everything will feel and be much better. Bailey knows better. By the time dinner is ready, the news report tab at the bottom of the TV screen reads,

## BODY OF TEENAGE GIRL FOUND IN UPTOWN ALLEY

By the ten o'clock news report, all the details are airing, but even before that, Delight's social media page was covered with condolences. The reports allow Bailey to freely express her sorrow wrapped in her mother's arms, but the painful itch in her chest worsens, leading her to the bathroom. As she rubs the top of her chest, she feels an outline protruding from her skin. Panicking, she yanks her V-neck cotton shirt away from her chest to discover what looks like a fang, the fang that was yanked from her mouth! The fang continues to move forward through the very top portion of her skin, until it finally settles, leveled as a part of her chest.

"No, no, no, no...Eric," she cries, not knowing what to do. She leaves the restroom, puts on her pajamas and lets her mom know she's going to bed, not wanting to talk to anyone.

For the days that follow, Bailey remains in seclusion until the day she must attend Delight's funeral, completely guilt-ridden as Delight's mother and many of Delight's relatives cry for the arrest of her murderer, the murderer of such a nice, beautiful young lady. After the funeral concludes, a distraught

Bailey returns to her house, changes clothes and leaves, going straight to Eric's home. He opens the door, and with tears flowing down her face, she makes a much needed request.

"Eric, take me to Tylon."

# THE END

THE SECOND BOOK of the BLACK FANG SERIES
COMING SOON
akirimpress.com | mirikacornelius.com

Black Fang